I0576012

COFFEE, SECRETS, CINCINNATI

A PARANORMAL STRUGGLE

JAMES CARL MEADOWS

COFFEE, SECRETS,
CINCINNATI
a paranormal struggle

Novel By

James Carl Meadows

Coffee, Secrets, Cincinnati

This is a work of fiction. The names, characters, locations, and incidents are either products of either fictitious creations of the author's imagination or are used fictitiously, and not to be construed as actual truthful representations of real-life persons, places, or events.

First Edition: June 2025

PCN: 9798992732801

LCCN: 2025905630

ISBN: 979-8-9927328-0-1 (paperback)

ISBN: 979-8-9927328-1-8 (ebook)

Thank you,

*To my wife, you are my rock and inspiration, my partner in all
things, and my Balm of Gilead.*
*To my sons, you are life and breath to me, the very handiwork of God,
a perfect gift, the apple of my eye.*
*To my friends, you are fonts of patience, faithful to deliver truth with
insight, and encouragement when the same is lacking.*

JAMES CARL MEADOWS

CHAPTER
ONE

He couldn't breathe. Pain racked his chest as he heaved and gasped, spitting out glass. A thick warm liquid dripped from his lips to his forehead. He squinted, unable to shield his eyes from the filtered shafts of sun. His heart raced, and head split, flushed with blood from sitting upside down. Desperately, he tried to pull himself free, but his body would not move. He hung, suspended between his seat and the ground by bindings. He touched them and remembered, his seatbelt. It wouldn't budge. He was stuck inside the mangled truck cab, and he could not free himself. Cries of pain and fear shrieked from his broken body.

Outside the crumpled cab, tromping feet rustled through the litter of leaves. Over the ringing inside his head, he heard a deep male voice. "My Lord and my God, please no, not both of them."

The man pushed his arm through the shattered passenger window and cleared thousands of clinging shards of glass from the bent frame. He craned his head through the distorted space.

"He's alive! The boy is still alive!"

"Help me!!!!" Jody squeezed out a vehement scream through his crushed chest.

"Look at me! Look at me! Right here, just look right here." The man beckoned Jody to focus on his eyes.

Jody looked, his body shaking, his mind still in a fog. Those eyes locked with his own. They were cold and grey at first, hints of blue and gold sparkled in the filtered shaft of sunlight. He fell into them, slipping slowly out of consciousness. Every time he blinked the darkness felt heavier and lingered longer around him. Each time they opened, he fell back into those steely blue pools, trying to forget where he was, the ugly horror of the macabre lingering inches away from his own wet and stinging skin.

Those steely blue eyes glistened with flecks of gold, glimmering in the sun. That glimmer grew into a glow, lending warm light to that tight, horrible space that imprisoned him. Those eyes held Jody, not in bonds, in an embrace, in the moment. They sustained him as he struggled not to break into a million pieces, drawing breath after painful breath.

"Stay with me." The man's voice begged. "Right here, stay right here, with me. Look in my eyes. I'm not going anywhere."

$\sim$

A dripping and steamy foot touched the cold linoleum floor. Jody emerged from the wet shower stall, slippery skin met slick steam-glazed flooring. Life's lessons were hard for Jody to learn. He was a very experiential learner, most happy and comfortable when trusting in his five senses to decipher the mysteries of the world around him. The physical rules of the universe made the world around him predictable and understandable. Unfortunately, just because those lessons could be learned, it did not always mean he would learn them. Such lessons came at him, in their most ruthless and hard to remember forms, when he was stressed or sleep deprived. This was one of those groggy and unfortunate mornings.

His right foot lost its grip on the slippery surface and his leg gave way. His heart leaped from his chest as he lunged toward the bathroom sink. Slippery hands hit the counter with a thud, and, although they strained, his fingers managed to maintain their hold on the hard rim. He braced himself against the stark white porcelain for a second. A solitary drop of hot shower water streamed down his furrowed brow, down his nose, falling freely through the air to meet the porcelain sink with a thunderous plop, accentuated by the sensory hyper focus brought on by his fight or flight response. The tectonic pressure of internal turmoil and present danger bent his perception of reality. Jody's mind's eye lent an ethereal pink tinge to the splattering water. For a moment, tiny crimson lines traced the course of draining water around the basin and down into the darkening drain. He blinked hard, struggling to catch his breath. He choked down a dull and distant terror from a life left miles and years behind him.

"I want you." A voice, sinister and soft, whirled around his ear.

He stopped breathing. It wasn't the first time he'd heard it. It was so familiar, in fact, he had named it. The snake. It whispered doubt and vile things Jody would never dare whisper. He felt it was his Id, that deep dark part of himself that represented his most dark and atavistic urges. He shoved it down and shook it out of his mind like so many times before.

Jody's reflection stared back at him through the steam glazed mirror. "Well, I didn't die. It can still be a good day."

The voice was his, but he wasn't sure he believed his own optimistic proclamation. Hardness, sadness, darkness followed him, like a shy black cat, peeking around every corner, darting past him in the shadows just beyond the perception of his peripheral vision.

"I didn't die," he repeated, swallowing hard, pushing down the nagging pangs of doubt and fear.

He stepped out of the bathroom. He needed to live in the now, to move, to breathe, to accomplish the millions of little tasks that needed to be done to make today a success.

Back on the more welcoming shaggy carpet of his bedroom, Jody fell to his knees and fished beneath the bed frame for one of his morning necessities, clothing. His unseen hand tapped the cold surface of a small metal box. He stopped, holding his breath.

"Leave it," he commanded himself sternly.

Two or three inches to the left, he found what he was looking for and pulled out a pair of blue jeans and a well wrinkled but relatively clean t-shirt. The terrible and ruthless nature of time forced him to capitulate and accept a certain disheveled nature in his appearance.

Time marched on, ruler of all, and blurred everything around him. Jody lost himself in his favorite morning radio station, mindlessly directing his ancient steed through the traffic of his daily commute, until, at last, he arrived at work, a quaint little storefront styled, like its neighbors on the humming Cincinnati street, in turn of the century architecture.

The huge windows in the storefront were partially papered with advertisement and announcement pages for special community events and band appearances along with the huge red and black name "The Study Hall" painted in script across each of the two great windowpanes. He swung open the wooden portal and was greeted by a familiar squeak, welcoming but at the same time foreboding.

It was eclectic, to say the least. In the front of the store was a coffee bar, adorned with all the gadgets and containers of multicolored, scented accoutrements of the trade surrounded by several spindly tables. On the opposite side, a red couch and some secondhand recliners and loveseats. In the back of the store were huge shelves filled with books of all kinds. Bookcases as tall as the ceiling lined each wall. The smell of coffee and old books permeated every ounce of air in the building.

A few people were already sitting, nursing warm coffees and tired magazines. Their faces were familiar, the smells and sounds comforting, but they brought no smile to Jody's face.

"Good morning, Jody," a delicate feminine voice greeted him from behind the coffee bar as he closed the door behind him.

He returned her greeting as he fought against an overwhelming sense of exhaustion. His voice strained to sound bright and cheery.

"You're almost late again," she retorted, in that familiar correcting schoolmarm tone.

Jody quickly pulled out a chair near the bar. "Just give me my normal morning jolt, Meg."

His eyes danced over her as she mixed his traditional morning double latte. His gaze performed a mesmerizing and slow circle all around her, catching quick glimpses of her beauty and then diverting his stare so as to avoid the perception of a creepy fixation. Dark, curly hair bounced on her sculpted, nearly bare, mocha-colored shoulders, while she busied herself with her task behind the bar. A maroon apron was dutifully tied over her traditional ensemble, which consisted of jeans and a crisply pressed wide necked dress shirt that accented her pleasant figure.

Meg looked up as she fastened the lid on his cup, and he caught a glimpse of the morning sun reflecting in her dark eyes. Jody basked for just a moment in their reflection before he suddenly became aware of himself. He was almost ashamed, filled with embarrassment, to have delved so completely in the adoration of her beauty that he lost his wits and withered into goo. She deserved better. He quickly diverted his eyes to the countertop.

"That'll be two dollars," she said.

He handed her two well-worn one-dollar bills. "Keep the change."

She stuffed them unceremoniously in the till and repaid his joke with half a smile. He took a couple of sips from his stout morning brew allowing the warm caffeinated liquid to percolate through his stiff muscles and into his foggy mind.

Ominous steps on the old hardwood floor steadily made their way from one of the back rooms to the coffee bar. Jody felt him before he could see him. The hair on the back of Jody's neck raised. Glancing over his shoulder, he beheld the face of an old man, gnarled by time, skin somehow simultaneously pallid and dark. The hair on the man's head was white and wispy, eyebrows thick and colored like salt and pepper. Time had pressed so hard against him, his eyes weary, dim, and cold.

"Good morning, Jody." The old man's voice was gravely and rusted from years of inhaling pipes and cigars. "Are you ready?" He didn't wait for Jody's reply. "Good, good. I've got a couple of new items in. I think they're quite interesting, and I know you can find a place for them. Follow me." The old man hobbled back toward a painted wooden door at the rear of the store labeled "Employees Only" and gestured for his young apprentice to follow.

Jody let his eyes fall one more time on the beautiful Meg. "I'll be around." She nodded in reply with a smile and continued busily to tend to customers ravenous for their morning caffeine fix.

The back room was hidden from view, like a dark family secret, tucked behind a constantly closed door painted to blend in with the rest of the wall. The masked threshold, once crossed, gave the hardy few who dared to explore there a sense of stale foreboding, part museum of a bygone era and part disheveled makeshift office. It was apparent that it once served a more domestic purpose, long forgotten in favor of commerce and progress.

In the far corner was an area set up for Mr. Tipton's desk, overflowing with papers and surrounded by a veritable fort of old file boxes and notebooks with a single drab green army surplus filing cabinet snuggly fitted into the very corner of the room. Another corner held a place for Jody's desk. It was smaller and only slightly less disheveled. Behind his desk sat a row of several more surplus filing cabinets. Near the door was an area devoted completely to stock items for the coffee bar. All the boxes, cans, and containers were stacked very neatly. This was in direct contrast to the opposite corner of the room, which was devoted to un-shelved books. It once had been neat and orderly. Nearest the wall, the books were stacked tidily in carefully ordered towers, but nearer the walkway the stacks became steadily more chaotic until it finally gave way to a virtual avalanche of literary art.

"I want you." The snake slithered inside Jody's mind, resonating between his ears.

"Stop it!" Jody exclaimed.

The old man stopped. "What?" His eyes thinned and voice quivered in confusion.

"Sorry, nothing Mr. Tipton. I was just remembering something."

"Well...um..." The old man's eyes trailed off toward his desk and he sputtered into silence.

There were no windows in the back room. The only natural sunlight that ever entered came from the large storefront windows during sunny summer days if the painted wooden door had been left open, and that rarely happened. It was always kept shut tight to keep customers from wandering in. The room was basked in an eerie yellow hue of aging incandescent bulbs. It was as if the oldness of the antique books had caused the very room itself to age and grow brittle.

Mr. Tipton had a seat in a swivel chair behind his heaping desk. "I put the boxes on your desk. They just came today from FedEx." He stretched, threw back his weary head and yawned. "Just do your usual magic. Catalogue them, check them for quality, and see if you can find a place for them on the shelves. Be sure there's no ripped or missing pages. I've never purchased from this guy before, but he gave a good price, so I thought I'd try him out."

Jody walked over to his desk, had a seat, and examined the two white parcels before him. He read the address label on the top of the first.

"Hey, this box says John Connoly"

"Yes, that's him."

"You bought a bundle of old dime store westerns off of him a couple of weeks ago. They were in pretty good shape."

"What?" the old man grumped. Mr. Tipton tried to search his mind for the event but could not seem to recall it. "Well... I believe you Jody. Just go ahead and check them out anyway." There was something off about the old man this morning. Normally, his mind was as good as a computer, able to spout off innumerable details concerning inventory and pricing. Today, he seemed slower, more distant and distracted, like his mind was becoming stale, his body scrunched over, muscles tight and hands trembling.

Jody took out his pocketknife and carefully cut the strong clear tape that bound the boxes together, delicately took out the books, and began his examination. He poured over the new delivery of books behind the tightly shut storeroom door.

The front room buzzed with activity. Many students, office workers, teachers, and even mothers with children in tow made their way into the shop. Each would go to Meg, place their order and patiently wait on them to be filled. While they waited some of them browsed the bookshelves, others read newspapers or magazines, and a few simply stared off into space contemplating last night's mistake or the promise that today may bring. Occasionally, one of those customers would come upon a book that intrigued them and take to Meg to buy along with their coffee. As Meg dutifully filled cups and rang up orders, the hands of the clock on the wall made their procession from 8:30 to 10:45, imperceptible to the people going about their business in The Study Hall.

Meg put the whipped cream on top of an espresso con panna for what seemed to be the millionth time. She looked up and noticed the line of people waiting to give their order had grown to four, and she had three other orders already waiting. "Mr. Dunkle, your espresso is ready." As she handed the man his coffee, she glanced at the clock. "Lunch rush, Billy, be on time for once."

A young man burst through the old wooden front door, his right hand waving in the air as if he wanted called on in the first grade. "I'm here. I'm here. Sorry, I know I'm late," he said in hurried tones.

"Again," Meg grumbled.

"Huh?" Bill asked pulling the white AirPods from his ears.

"You're late again." Meg was stern. Bill had tried her patience too many times in the past to be given much grace. It was not the first time he was late and she felt unless she made a big deal out of the whole situation it would certainly not be the last.

Bill donned his apron and quickly began prepping his cash register. "Maybe if this place wasn't as cold as a tomb all the time it wouldn't give me the creeps and I'd want to get here early like that crazy guy."

Jody didn't have to look up as he busily shelved countless paperback books. He knew Billy was talking about him.

"I have a Chemistry test this afternoon that I stayed up until 3am studying for. Then, when I woke up, my roommate's dog was clawing on the door to get out again, more scratches.

The apartment manager is going to love that. Why they let dogs in that place is beyond me. But then, when I let the dog out, he ran straight down the street to that old yellow fire hydrant in front of Mr. Spitzer's building and you can guess who..."

"Billy," Meg interjected.

"What?" He nearly dropped a whole stack of empty cups on the floor in shock.

"I don't care. Help the customers."

"Oh, yeah," he recovered. "Thanks for coming, sir. How can I help you today?" Billy's disheveled appearance and dutiful smile might have been endearing to some, but not to Meg. It only hardened her misgivings about his unprofessional behavior.

Jody emerged from the back room with a stack of freshly catalogued and checked books cradled in his hands. He scanned the fiction section and found an opening in just the right spot three shelves up and slid two lightly used books in place. His eyes looked to the top shelves one stack over. "Ah, perfect, a high-rise vacancy in the horror section." He grabbed the sliding ladder, moved it into place, and began his ascent. Nearly to the top, the book slipped from his hand and landed on the floor with a thud. Time stopped in the tiny shop and all eyes snapped to the source of the sound.

"Quick, Meg, could you give me a hand please?" Jody whispered as loudly as he could, trying not to alarm their boss.

It was too late. The door to the back room burst open with a loud swoosh. Mr. Tipton glared at Jody as the young man clung to the ladder, still as a statue, a trembling finger still outstretched silently begging Meg to pick up the fallen book. The old man did not scold him. He had never raised his voice to Jody in all the years they had worked together, but he looked at him through heavy, downturned eyebrows that bellowed of fatherly disappointment. With a muffled harumph, Mr. Tipton disappeared back behind the door. Jody gulped as the normal buzz of conversations began again.

"Oh, sure." She wiped the residue of recently dashed cinnamon from her hands with a barely controlled smirk and walked over to Jody's belated rescue. She bent down to fetch the book for Jody, an action that accented her young feminine form in her denim jeans. Her elegantly arching frame did not go unnoticed by Bill. He promptly overfilled a cup of coffee and scalded his hand.

"Crap!" he exclaimed, wiping his hand with the cold bar cloth. Jody looked over his shoulder to see the commotion, and Billy pointed semi-discretely and mouthed "Dude, she is so hot." To which Jody replied with a stern look and a head shake.

"Here you go," Meg stretched and reached the book up to Jody.

"Thanks."

"Wait," she said, reading aloud the faded red lettering on the yellow cover. "Dracula by Bram Stoker. I think I'll take this one."

Jody rolled his eyes and whispered, "Not this time, this one is from 1897. It's worth $20,000. The old man didn't pay anywhere near that much for it, but it's well out of your price range."

"I could buy it," Meg said defiantly.

"Yeah, if you didn't eat for a year." Jody felt the heft of the old tome as it shifted completely from her possession to his.

"What is he doing shelving this thing anyway?" Meg asked.

"You know Mr. Tipton. I told him all about the value and he told me to put a good dust cover on it and shelve it. 'I'm running an antique bookstore not a museum,' he said. He wouldn't imagine tucking it away in the back. We need a good glass case that's what we need." Carefully, very carefully, he put it in its place and descended the ladder to return to his long list of clerical duties.

The lunch rush continued. Meg soldiered through it, keeping one eye on her customers and one eye on Bill trying to make sure that his mind remained focused on his official duties. At two o'clock Meg washed her hands one final time and hung up her apron. "I'm out for the day boys," she said loud enough she was sure Mr. Tipton could hear her from the back room. "I've got a Psychology exam at three. Wish me luck!"

"I want you." The snake hissed again.

Billy gave Meg a half-hearted grunt of acknowledgement as she sauntered out onto the sidewalk. Jody discretely admired her mysterious beauty through the windowpane as he made his way to his station at the espresso machine. She paused in front of the storefront. Jody watched her dark shoulders rise and fall as she breathed in deeply shooting an uneasy stare back in his direction. She took a single step, still searching for something behind her, but never making eye contact with Jody. Then, the beautiful young woman turned and marched away into the press of the city with a telling urgency.

"Did she hear that?" Jody mumbled to himself.

CHAPTER
TWO

The old wooden grandfather clock in the front of the store rang out the hour with seven golden tones. It was one of Jody's favorite sounds, but it also meant something Jody was not ready for, the end of the workday. Without work, there were no distractions from the horrible voice that hounded him. He was bombarded by doubts, insecurities, and uncertainties.

He had no post-college plan, not really. The uncharacteristic lack of a plan gnawed at him. He would have to move back home if he couldn't find a job, a real job that paid a respectable salary. Going back to Virginia felt like the worst possible move he could make. Home wasn't home for him anymore. It held none of the nostalgic draw found by so many of his classmates. His apartment was home, his friends, the crowded Cincinnati streets, were all home to him now. They held him fast, secure, and welcomed him every day. Virginia was void, without meaning or even the slightest prospect of finding fulfillment.

An uncontrollable current of fear and doubt was already taking him down into deep-seeded trenches of self-loathing. Work was his life vest, protection against a watery grave.

Simple tasks, smiling faces, all helped numb the pain of things he wanted left far behind him, at home. People, they were what mattered to Jody, and Cincinnati held plenty of them.

Though Cincinnati was home, the four walls of the Study Hall never quite felt like a sanctuary to him. It was oddly off-putting. There was something about it he couldn't quite put his finger on. It left him uneasy. Perhaps the dark and dank corners were holding on to the sorrow of countless passersby, painful emotions, never quite vanquished by the steamy aroma of designer coffees.

"It's seven Jody," Mr. Tipton grumbled with his deep guttural manner. "Shouldn't you be off somewhere doing something else with your spring evening?"

Jody swallowed hard. "No." His sheepish voice whistled through parched lips.

Mr. Tipton sat back heavily in his chair and sighed. It was intended to be a sigh, but it sounded more like a growl. Weathered and trembling hands took a folded white handkerchief from his right back pocket, carefully removed his spectacles, dabbed his furrowed brow, examined the lenses, and placed them once again firmly upon his nose.

Jody shook himself. "Oh, um, no, not today. I've got a lot of work to do and I'm already done with my exams for the semester."

"Life is precious, Jody, and youth even more precious still." The old man coughed into the back of his hand. "It's not right for a young man like yourself to be cooped up here in a dim, smelly room when there are better things to do."

Jody looked down and tried to busy his hands in his work. "I appreciate the advice, sir, but I really don't have anything else to do. All of my friends are busy. My family, well, let's just say they're a bit too busy to have me tagging along at the moment."

"Off on vacation?"

"Yes, again, this time a cruise in the Bahamas." In fact, this was their third vacation this year. His mom had gotten remarried 9 months ago, and they had taken several trips since. Jody just assumed they were enjoying some kind of extended honeymoon, but that honeymoon never stopped. They made a habit of being somewhere else almost every holiday since they started dating. Any time Jody would have expected to be able to come home to smiles and warm food on the table, he would travel home to find frozen dinners and quiet contemplation in front of the television set.

"Ah, yes, quite lovely this time of year, I'm sure." It was a stilted attempt at sincerity. Jody couldn't tell if he meant it or not, but in the end it didn't matter.

Jody didn't like to talk much about his mother and stepfather. "Besides, I have made it my personal mission to see that," he pointed at the now slightly smaller mountain of unorganized books, "is no longer a thorn in your side before I leave for the summer."

Mr. Tipton chuckled from deep within his throat, "That, my boy, has been sitting there in one form or another for the last twenty-five years. I don't suspect it remaining another few months will pain me too much."

"But none-the-less, sir, I would like to see it gone. I would consider it a personal accomplishment."

The aging Mr. Tipton pulled himself up from his chair with some considerable effort and stretched. His hands began to involuntarily tremble. He clasped them together and fidgeted. The fingers of his right hand played with the digits on his left with a sense of mindless uncertainty.

"The bones of this old house... are all old and rotting," He mumbled half under his breath voice quivering. A cough rattled his weary chest as he gathered his wits about him. His voice rang out clearer, louder, more determined. "And I would like to see you gone, somewhere, anywhere else, so I can have some peace."

That right hand mesmerized Jody. It seemed to have a mind of its own. Jody could sense a pattern. In just a few quiet moments, he discerned a focus. Its fingers paid special attention to the old man's peculiarly unmarked ring finger. There was no tan line, no deep furrowed crevasse etched into the flesh outlined by timeworn callouses. The finger was pristine and, in every way, the same as every one of his other digits.

"A man ages when he sits behind a desk, in certain ways, different than his fellow travelers that are not bound to such a leisurely lifestyle." Mr. Tipton walked over to his young employee and placed his hand on Jody's desk. "His joints stiffen, his muscles ache, and he cowers like a roach scurrying from the bright sun in the heat of the day. Young legs are better used chasing after beauty, and young arms better holding it close."

"Now, Mr. Tipton...," Jody half-heartedly protested. The truth of Mr. Tipton's words stirred him somehow, deep down in a place Jody had hoped could be avoided just a little longer.

The old man stood upright and hobbled over to the coat rack. He took down the brown fedora that had served him for decades and placed it firmly upon his head. With his right hand he retrieved an old black cane crowned with a molded silver dog's head, which he only had to use until his joints became accustomed to the motions of walking after a long day in his chair. He tapped the silver dog to the brim of his hat.

"Remember, books can keep the mind sharp, but when the lights go out and you lay your head upon your pillow, knowledge alone is poor comfort."

Jody took well his subtle meaning. "Goodnight, Mr. Tipton," His lips upturned in a halting smile at the strange corpse of a man. Somehow this tired and wrinkled frame, quaking before him, managed to exude more prescient and fatherly advice than his own stepfather had for years.

"Goodnight young man." Mr. Tipton hobbled toward the door of their ancient cave and turned as he opened it. "The night shift will be locking up for you tonight as usual. Do try not to stay here too long. Get some rest."

"I will, sir."

"You know Jody," the old man said, wagging the end of his cane in Jody's direction, "you've been working for me for, what, four years now?"

"Five, sir."

"Five years, and you have been the hardest working employee I have ever had. I truly appreciate you. I want you to know that. Just try to remember to live."

"Thank you, sir. I will, sir." They were grateful but empty words. Jody didn't really know how to live. He abhorred leisure. He knew how to work, how to lose himself in tasks and goals. This exaggerated work ethic had served him well in school and he preferred to trust in its familiarity as he transitioned into life in the real world.

Mr. Tipton continued out into the evening sunlight and walked, in his halting manner, on his way home. Jody shut the door and went back to work in his quiet room. In a twinkling of an eye, the old clock out front tolled the ninth hour. Jody rose from his cataloguing to check on the front-line closers.

He opened the door to find a beautiful smiling face staring at him from a nearby table.

"Hello there stranger." The greeting dripped warmly from fiery red lips. The young woman lowered a well-loved porcelain mug to the high-top table, crowned with traces of her ruby lipstick. Her flowing red hair seemed almost translucent in the dim yellow lamplight.

"Hello." Jody was shocked to be so warmly addressed by a

beautiful woman. Normally he was quite invisible to the opposite sex. "Didn't I see you..."

"Yesterday...yes." She finished his sentence and pulled her leather purse strap over her bare shoulder. "You were showing someone how to clean the espresso machine when I spilled my espresso all over the table."

"Oh yeah!"

"Thank you by the way. You didn't have to clean all that up by yourself."

Jody motioned for the young man behind the counter to start closing up. "It's the least I could do. Glad I was able to help." He extended a slightly sweaty palm. "Oh, um, my name is Jody by the way. I'm sorry, you are?"

"Karen."

There was something familiar about this woman. Jody just couldn't identify it. It intrigued him, drew him in like a long-forgotten mystery. He had to know more.

"Are you making us part of your nightly routine?"

She looked one last time over her shoulder, scanning the thinning crowd for a familiar face. "No, just looking for a friend. Looks like he's not here tonight." She quickly grabbed her mug and placed it in the bin, pausing only long enough to offer Jody a nod and a fleeting wave of her sleek, feminine hand.

"Goodnight." Jody's voice trailed off, giving chase to the mysterious young woman. He never quite knew if it caught up to her as the door ringer faithfully chimed, marking her exit. Jody rubbed his cheek, feeling the rough stubble of his growing five o'clock shadow. The night barista said his goodbyes and Jody was left alone with his thoughts and the haunting ticking of the old grandfather clock.

Jody turned off the lights to the store front and slipped through the hidden door into the back office. A cold and damp chill settled into his bones from the still air of the back room. It was a now familiar feeling, being alone, but not alone, here in the bowels of an ancient building that felt more of tomb than remodeled row house. He had to focus. He was on a mission, conquer the mountain of books within the next week. Nothing would stand in his way.

His pattern did not waiver. First, he approached the stack and grabbed a book from the top. Then he would flip through the book and look for any obvious damage. If it was damaged too much, he would throw it into the box marked trash. If it wasn't too badly damaged, he would note any flaws in the computer cataloguing program along with the identifying info for the book. Then he would carefully thumb through each page to make sure none were missing. If a book passed that inspection, then it was rated, priced, listed online and then shelved.

Jody did this sixteen times after Karen left. His eyelids began to feel very heavy. He tried to revive himself with more and more sips from his now cooling coffee, but to no avail. As he looked at page 156 of his seventeenth book, he slumped in his chair and the world became dark and warm.

Dong, dong, dong. Golden tones rang out from the old grandfather clock. Jody awoke, his heart racing.

"Ow!" he exclaimed attempting to move his now quite stiff neck.

It was three a.m., the witching hour. A chill ran down Jody's spine and his whole body shook. He knew not whether it was his body quickly rising from its slumber or the memory of a hundred books about unsuspecting victims tormented at this loathsome hour, when the veil between the here and now and the beyond grew its thinnest.

Jody steeled his nerves and his skin ceased quaking. He looked over at the mountain of books, the very symbol of failure of discipline to a simple bookstore's clerk. It didn't look as intimidating as it had before, perhaps only half as imposing as it was when he started chipping away at it five years ago, but every inch spoke of tasks overlooked and time used unwisely to Jody.

"I will beat you," he said scolding the pile of crumbling tomes.

He would not see another shipment of orders added to the pile before it was annihilated. He quickly looked at his calendar. The next order was due to arrive in four days.

"You are going down. This week!" he exclaimed, shaking his finger at the silent mound.

If he hoped to conquer this gargantuan task, he had to stay awake. His eyes darted hurriedly about the room looking for anything that would add energy to his bland environment and keep him functioning. His gaze fell on an old record player near Mr. Tipton's desk. The old man sometimes entertained himself by listening to selections from his ancient collection of records. The rise and fall of music seemed to dictate the tone and attitude of the old man's workday.

That leaning tower of records was like Mr. Tipton's church, where he quietly went day in and day out to find inspiration and wrestle with unseen demons deep within the hidden recesses of his mind. He never spoke of the struggles, but Jody could see the storm raging behind his boss' weathered eyes as each day waxed long and each task grew harder.

Jody approached the tower with soft and measured steps in awe and reverence befitting the honor bestowed upon each record by his mentor. He walked over and delicately pulled the first record from the top of the tilting stack beside the player. Carefully, with the most supreme attention to detail, Jody slid the record onto the turntable and set the needle as it spun. The old vinyl creaked and popped and began to play its music.

"Marvin Gaye?" Jody asked himself, with his mouth contorted like it had just tasted too sour lemonade.

Jody chuckled. It was not quite what he had come to expect from Mr. Tipton's taste, but somehow apropos given their earlier conversation, an auditory carpe diem poem left behind to spur Jody on to enjoy the more pleasureful pursuits in life. There would be time for all of that later. For now, there was only his fast-approaching deadline and the abhorrent, unsightly mountain of disheveled books. He sat back down and started to work. He was on a mission, all he had to fight was the sultry draw of sleep, and the icy fingers of the occasional draft gnawing at his bones.

CHAPTER
THREE

A piercing ringtone tore through the stale air of the back room like a lightning bolt. Jody groped around the top of his desk trying to find his phone. Finally, his hand landed on it and he held it up to his face as it vibrated in his palm. The screen flashed the name in letters from his contacts list so big Jody could read it even in his groggy state, "Billy- Probably late."

"Hello," he said in a cracking voice through his dry mouth.

"Hey dude, where are you?" the garbled voice of Bill Johnston yelled at him through the tiny speakers placed up to his ears.

"What? Billy? What do you want?" Jody asked still confused.

"I called your place and you weren't there. Where are you man?"

"I'm, I'm at the store Billy what do you want?" Jody stuttered.

"What? What are you doing there? Do you know what time it is?"

"No. No, I don't. Do you?"

"It's four thirty in the morning man. You've got to get out of there a.s.a.p. The old man gets there at 6 and he'll kill you if he finds out you're sleeping there."

Jody snapped to attention. Mr. Tipton must never find out he was at the shop all night. He was immediately aware of the repetitive thumping of the record player and went over to it to turn it off and put the record back.

"What do you want Billy? Why are you calling me at four thirty in the morning?"

"I need you to come get me man."

"What? What are you talking about?"

"I can't drive, man. I need you to come pick me up."

"What? Where at? Where are you Billy?" Jody turned off the lights in the back room and headed for the door.

"I'm at Helen's place man."

"Get her to take you wherever it is you need to go then. Don't bother me about it." Jody shut the front door behind him and made sure it latched.

"No man I can't. I'm in her yard. She kicked me out man."

"What?"

"I totally rocked out on my Chemistry final, right? And so, I decided to go out and have some fun with some friends. I got a little tipsy and..." A muffled thud and airy swishes replaced Billy's voice for a moment. "Crap! Sorry man, I dropped the phone...tripped over a dang water hose."

"A little tipsy? When did you stop drinking?"

"I don't know like two or something. Then I had one of the guys take me over to Helen's house. She let me in and everything was going fine then like twenty minutes ago she throws me my shirt and says 'Get out, get out now, and don't come back.'"

"What happened?" Jody asked breathlessly as he ran toward his car, hoping Mr. Tipton hadn't decided to come in extra early for whatever reason and wouldn't see him.

"I don't know man. I can't remember anything. I must have said something."

"You think?" Jody said sarcastically. "Look dude, I'm wiped, just call a cab or something."

"I can't man. I left my wallet in there and I'm not going back in to get it."

"Oh, come on." Jody pleaded in disbelief.

"She was screaming at me man and shoving me out the door. I am not knocking on that door dude."

Jody reached his car and fumbled with the keys and hopped in.

"Fine. I'll be there in 10 minutes."

He sped out of the parking garage and onto the street. The tires squalled. He floored it until he was three or four blocks away from the store where he finally allowed himself to slow down and took a deep breath. Jody vented his frustration into the empty cab that surrounded him, mumbling expletives under his breath, finally reaching a crescendo with a very loud "I'm not going to get a speeding ticket for you Billy, not again."

Within fifteen minutes he pulled in front of Helen Gudtzi-et's house. It was a small but beautiful brownstone home. The yard was immaculately tended, and the hedges perfectly trimmed, a work of domestic art, which could even be appreciated by streetlight. Helen was like that, very well-kept and well-rounded. Organization and cleanliness were nearly her religion. Billy was the exact opposite, and there he sat at the end of her driveway looking like he had just been in a bar fight and weeping like a little boy who lost his puppy.

Billy wiped the tears from his face trying to save his dignity as he saw Jody pull up next to him.

Jody rolled down the windows. "Get in"

"What took you so long dude?"

"Get in." Jody repeated sternly. "You called me at four-thirty in the morning and want to know what took me so long? You really are a piece of work, you know that?"

Billy got in and fumbled with his seatbelt. "Look I'm sorry man. I'm…just…just take me home man."

Jody took off with his pitiful passenger head in hand beside him. "You reek man. Did you drink that stuff or wallow in it? Ugh and you smell like vomit too. Do you have vomit on your clothes? Did you just get vomit on my seats?" Jody was becoming ever more impatient.

"No man, look, I don't know. I just don't know. Just take me home ok. I don't need this 'I'm better than you' speech right now, ok."

"And Helen? Little five foot two Helen with the brown doe eyes? Little timid Helen who I have never seen try to raise her voice my whole life, she kicked you out, screaming? What did you do?"

"Look, dude I don't know, ok. I don't know." He belched up a noxious concoction of liquor fumes and held it in his mouth, trying not to vomit all over Jody's dashboard.

The remainder of the twenty-minute drive to Billy's apartment passed silently. The curves and turns brought no closure for Jody and not much more clarity to his passenger. It did, however, bring the first crimson fingers of sunshine on the horizon followed by a wash of light and morning color.

Billy reached for the beauty of the early morning sunrise, pressing his fingers softly against the window. "Dude, don't you ever get scared of stuff while you're in that place?"

Jody's face whipped back in Billy's direction. "What?… What are you talking about?"

"The store, man. I mean you're there all the time and sleep there sometimes and stuff. I just figured, you know…". His voice trailed off and another noxious burp slipped through his lips. "… That maybe you would have seen somethin' by now… anything… anything? Nothin'? Ok, man, that's cool."

Jody glanced back and forth between his drunk friend and the road. "What are you... You know what, you are so drunk. I can't believe you even..."

Billy squinted, "Dude, this is it, ok you can stop."

Jody pulled his car to the curb in front of Billy's building. Billy didn't have to remind him, he knew the path to Billy's place like the back of his hand. "Do you have your keys with you?" he asked dutifully.

Billy fumbled around in his pockets until his hands finally emerged jingling a small pair of silver keys on a black and red University of Cincinnati Bearcats fob. "I've got 'em."

"Get out and go sleep it off. I'll cover for you this morning." Jody said with just a slight hint of understanding.

"Dude I can..."

"You are so drunk you can barely walk. Go in and sleep it off, Billy." Jody allowed his irritation to show through his voice.

"I'm supposed to start at eight 'cus it's the weekend."

"Got it. Just remember I'm saving your rear-end here Billy. Mr. Tipton won't put up with this kind of stuff long."

Bill opened the door and started to get out. "And dude, if, if you could call Helen for me..."

"Get out Billy! Sleep it off!"

Jody watched his friend stumble up to the door of his first-floor apartment and make his way inside. He opened his mouth and strained his face in a silent scream swatting repeatedly at the peeling faux leather steering wheel. Jody hated over the top displays of emotion, but Billy had driven him to the brink more than once.

Bill was the kind of friend his mother had always called a bad influence, but he had known Billy since high school. When the rest of the world spent an entire summer telling Jody "I'm sorry for your loss", Billy handed him a beer and an open ear. The hand of fate had pushed them both North to Cincinnati for college, and Jody was truly thankful. Billy had been there for him at his worst and at his best, so he would be there for Billy, always.

Jody drove home, another ten minutes back in the direction of work. The calming colors of the rising morning sun and his copious lack of sleep wore him down. The sounds from the radio wafted back and forth around his nodding head. The song warped and warbled like a well-worn record dancing listlessly on a turntable.

He was drifting softly into sleep. His eyes bleary, the colors of the world muddled into one another behind a white and milky haze. Ahead, on the shoulder of the road, stood the silhouette of a tall, block shouldered man in a raincoat. He could feel the wheel pulling, fighting against his guidance, beckoning him toward the dark figure. His foot felt heavy. He didn't have the strength to lift it from the accelerator. He wanted to scream, wanted to cry out, but he couldn't catch his breath.

Without warning, the blare of an oncoming car horn tore him from his sleepy state. The terrified face of a white haired, well-tanned grandfather gawked at him behind the bug splattered windshield of a late model convertible. Tires squealed as Jody yanked the steering wheel just in time to avoid the collision. His tires began to spin out of control as they tried in vain to bite into the loose gravel on the shoulder of the road. Jody grappled with the wheel, fighting it this way and that as he struggled to regain control. The car stopped, and as the frame rocked back and forth, it was engulfed in a cloud of dust. He breathed hard and fast. His chest hurt, like his heart was being ripped out with an unseen bare hand. He cried out trying to control his physical reaction, but it was too late. He screamed in agony, hot tears streaming down his cheeks.

"No, no, no!"

Shaking arms and hands pounded the steering wheel. He could not help it. He lost all control. He was back there, reliving what happened so many years ago. Scenes from that terrifying night flashed through his mind's eye in choppy, jarring clips, past intertwined with present, flashing so rapidly that he lost all orientation in space and time.

Hunched over, he hugged the steering wheel with all of his might like a life preserver. Sharp, rhythmic knocking pounded in his ears, drawing his feet firmly back into the present. He looked to his window and saw the stubbly face of a police officer peering back at him through the glass, beckoning him with hand motions to roll his window down. Jody complied. The officer asked him a question, but all Jody could hear was an echoing voice in his head repeating, "I have to open the store!"

CHAPTER
FOUR

Saturday morning hurt. Everything hurt; Jody's pride, his head. Pangs of regret racked his mind and body. He shouldn't have worked so long. He shouldn't have been driving so late. He shouldn't have fallen asleep at the wheel.

Meg threw a maroon apron at him as he stepped over the threshold into work. Jody looped it over his head and read the lapel as he tied the strings behind his back. "Billy? Really, I have to wear his apron too? I take it you heard."

"Oh, I heard alright. Missy called me after she saw you pick Billy up at the curb last night." Meg followed up her comment with a wet and soapy rag thrown unceremoniously at Jody's head. "Did I ever tell you how I hate late night phone calls? I need my sleep."

Jody wiped the splatter from his eyes and proceeded to give the tables a quick morning wash. "No argument from me."

Meg winced. His tone, the way he carried himself, all spoke volumes to her about her long-time friend.

"Are you okay?" There was no reply, but none was needed. "It happened again, didn't it?" He continued to focus on his work and said nothing. "Jody, listen to me. It happened again. Are you alright? What happened?"

"Nothing."

Meg marched around the counter and sat down at the table right in front of him. "Something happened. Don't you lie to me, Jody Howard."

Jody's eyes darted over to the old grandfather clock. "We've got fifteen minutes until we open. There's no time for this."

Meg snatched the rag from his hand mid-wipe. "Nothing else is happening, Jody, until you sit down and talk to me."

"Okay. Okay. Yes, it happened again."

"Sit." Her finger extended out like a sword drawn in anger.

"I already told you. Yes. It happened. We don't..."

"Sit, down, now!"

Jody complied. He hated weakness. He had spent the entirety of his young adult years trying to overcome it. The last thing he wanted to do was waste time talking about the debilitating flashbacks that plagued him.

"Where did it happen?"

"In the car."

"The car!? You were driving? Jody, that's terrible. Did you wreck?"

"I didn't wreck the car." Jody's finger tapped nervously on the table top as he looked back at the clock again. "I fell asleep at the wheel, and almost hit a guy, and I got the car to stop on the side of the road and then..."

Meg pushed her hand across the table and gently held him by the finger he had been tapping. Jody recoiled and pulled it from her grasp.

"Jody, that's terrible. Have you..."

"I'm going to call my therapist right after my shift." Jody looked at the clock again, stood up, and started to pace nervously. "I didn't get any sleep. I don't know how long I was there. The cops came by and checked on me. I had to do the whole sobriety test and everything."

"You need to rest." She walked over to him and tried to hold his attention as his eyes skittered around the room. "You need to process. Why don't you..."

"...After my shift." He pointed at the old wooden clock. "It's almost time. Please, let's just get this day over with."

Meg conceded.

Emotions sloshed back and forth in Jody's chest like a stormy sea. His feelings rocked back and forth wildly all morning. At moments he was almost peaceful, at others depressed. Working was difficult, emotionally and physically.

Perhaps Meg was correct. Maybe he should just fold up the apron, leave it on the table, and go home to sleep until the world made better sense. She cared. She always wanted what's best for him. It was endearing, except for when it counted the most, in the heat of the moment, then, it felt overbearing. For now, she was endearing again.

The one truly bright spot of the day for him was getting to spend time with Meg behind the counter. It was exhilarating trying to remember the barista craft he hung up almost two years ago when he took on the mantle of Mr. Tipton's clerk. The rush and rhythm of the morning crowd, all the new faces, becoming reacquainted with a few old regulars he had forgotten all about, mingled with awkward conversation with a member of the female sex.

It was not just conversation with a member of the female sex, but conversation with the only woman he even cared to pay attention to for the last three years. Her smiles triggered his own, her laughter spurred his own. The slightest incidental touch of her hand to his in the bustle of the morning rush sent cold waves of goosebumps up his arm.

Years of experience taught him what to expect from his beautiful counterpart. Jody knew Meg, learned who she was, how she thought, all her motivations and her hang-ups. She learned the same about him. They worked well together. He twirled a drying towel around the inside of a bone white coffee mug. She was not perfect, but as he stole another glance at her beautiful face in the golden shafts of morning sun, he found himself contented to overlook those minor flaws. No one was perfect, especially not him. He wondered if he was worthy of the same small grace as he placed the mug back up on the shelf behind the counter.

The hidden door in the rear of the store creaked. Mr. Tipton shuffled out and closed it carefully behind him. A cold draft crawled across the coffee bar. It ran up Jody's bare arms and caused every hair on the back of his head to raise on end. He looked up at Meg. She visibly shivered and backed away from the counter, pretending to check the level of coffee beans in the grinders.

The old man walked to the center of the room and stopped, carefully surveying the spines of the books along the top shelves through tilted spectacles. The downturned corners of his dry, cracking lips grew to a Mona Lisa smile and a low growl reverberated from his chest.

Arising from anonymity, someone stood from a table and approached Mr. Tipton, catching Jody's eye. His countenance glowed. He had a thick black beard that grew down his chest like a well-groomed topiary. His head was bald, freshly shaven. His skin was light, not pasty but pallid in a way that asked for a few more hours of sun. He was dressed well, pressed blue jeans and a simple t-shirt covered by a navy-blue suit coat. His eyes seemed kind, and his demeanor decried a welcoming confidence. Dancing inside the blue orbs Jody saw the flickering flames of a passion and the focus of determined purpose.

The mysterious man extended a hand toward Mr. Tipton. The greeting was left unrequited, returned only with a grumbling, "Well?"

The bearded man asked if they could do business in the back, which was promptly and rudely refused. "No, you're not going back there ever again, and I don't care if you ever come back at all."

With downturned face and rounded shoulders, the bearded man reached deep into his pocket and handed over a folded stack of cash after removing it from a silver clip. Mr. Tipton countered by shoving a leather-bound antique book into his mysterious counterpart's empty hands and turning with no further words spoken.

The bald and bearded man glanced over at Jody on his way out. He paused, mouth agape, as if he wanted to say something but at the last moment gathered his faculties and restrained his impulse. He continued through the store with downturned eyes and said nothing more.

Jody bumped Meg's arm as he moved about making another coffee, causing her to jostle a half-opened metal cylinder of roasted coffee beans. She caught it just in time, before it fell from the shelf. Meg looked up and tried to find the old man again, but he had gone in a blink of an eye. The door to the backroom shut with a rush and a thud.

Jody shook himself. It seemed almost unnatural that an old man could move so quickly out of sight. He could hear Mr. Tipton mumbling something behind the thin wall about 'stupid modern music'. The shrill groan of a record needle unceremoniously thrust into its course echoed through the Study Hall, followed by loud and mournful music.

"There!" Mr. Tipton's voice filtered through the walls to Jody's still shocked ears. "That's much better." He moaned and groaned like a great beast settling into a well-deserved hibernation.

"It's just so... creepy." Meg's voice trailed off as Jody turned to pour another drink.

"The music?" he replied. "I know, but it's his favorite. You'd think he could go one day without playing that blasted record."

"It's not just the music." She stopped and wiped sweat from

her forehead with the back of her hand. "It's Mr. Tipton, this old building, it's everything."

The voice of a familiar customer drew Jody's attention back to the counter. "Hey, Jody, wasn't expecting to see you here today."

Roger was the consummate musician with a unique character all his own, and he dressed to match his personality. Crowning his soft brow was a lightly colored fedora with a flashing red feather. On his thin shoulders hung a sport coat of camelhair, by its looks, tailored circa 1968. He had picked it up at a local goodwill for what he considered a steal at $1.50.

"Good day Meg." He leaned over the counter and scanned the menu.

"Happy Saturday." She sank deep into Roger's cold steely eyes as they moved slowly across the words posted on the wall behind her. He placed his order, which she dutifully filled.

"Hey Jody, my band is playing the Blind Lemon tonight. We start about eight. Stop by and give us a listen. I think you'll like some of the new stuff we've been working on."

"Maybe I will." Jody replied with a smile.

Rodger picked his donut off the plate with one hand and his coffee with the other. He took a warm delicious bite into his sugary confection and with a wink and a nod toward Meg, headed back out the door.

"You're heading over to Mt. Adams tonight?" Meg mocked

"I'm thinking about it." he answered flatly. "I could use some good music and a nice atmosphere away from this place. Would you like to come with me?"

"I don't know, maybe." Meg rang up another customer and flashed Jody her best sideways shy smile. "Local cover bands have never quite been my thing, but tonight... maybe."

Jody wanted her to say yes, more than anything in the world. He started to use the assumptive approach. "When should I..."

"If I'm not there by 8, don't bother keeping my seat saved. It does sound like fun though." Meg was nothing if not hard to read.

Mr. Tipton's voice called from behind the old wooden door. "Can I see you for a moment please, Mr. Howard?"

"Coming Mr. Tipton." Jody wiped his hands and threw off his borrowed smock. Meg looked at him inquisitively, and Jody simply shrugged his shoulders. The mysterious door creaked open and he stepped into a world filled with the strains of violin music and the smell of old books. "What can I do for you, sir?"

"Pull up a chair Jody." The old man gestured, his voice moving with the music with a strange sing-song quality.

Jody grabbed the swivel chair from behind his own desk and scooted it over to Mr. Tipton's. He sat down and waited a moment for Mr. Tipton to stop the task he was completing. The old man raised a thick peppery eyebrow and began to speak. "You're a good friend Jody, covering for Billy today."

"Thank you, sir."

"Your friend there has had some pretty spotty performance. Luckily, he called you up. That shows some kind of ownership and responsibility, I suppose."

"Yes, sir." Jody knew his friend hadn't called, hadn't even asked very politely, but even though Bill was a self-absorbed idiot sometimes, it didn't mean he didn't deserve a job.

"You, though, Jody, have excellent initiative, and don't think I haven't noticed the way you've shepherded Billy along, gently pulling him, coaching him. You've got the instincts of a great manager."

"Thank you, sir."

A sly smile grew across the old man's face as he twirled his spectacles in his hand, holding them in his fingers by the earpieces. "I've noticed you've made progress on that pile of books you've been tackling. How late were you here last night anyway?"

Jody paused for a moment, not wanting to say the wrong thing. He didn't want to lie. "Fairly late, but I still got some sleep."

"Good, good." Mr. Tipton fumbled around on his desk clearing it so he could see his full size desk calendar. "So, when was it exactly that you were heading back down to Virginia?"

"I was planning on heading out a week from Monday, sir, if that's ok with you?"

"Oh, yes." The old man nodded. He searched his calendar and wrote something down on Monday the following week. "I wouldn't dream of keeping a young man like yourself from seeing his parents." He looked up at Jody over the rim of his glasses. "I know you've been working hard, and I expect you not to show up tomorrow."

"But sir, I..."

"Tomorrow is Sunday. You've already been here six days this week. Take the day off. Go to church, go to a theme park, sleep, I don't care what you do, just don't do it here."

"I really think..."

"That is my order to you as an employee." Mr. Tipton scolded. "Rest tomorrow. If you show up here tomorrow, it will be a danger to your prospective future employment." His firm face wavered, and his smile cracked. "Someone once told me that there is a war over your soul, your very being. Only you can decide who wins that war. Only you can decide who wins. Decide who wins, Jody. Let it be you. Don't just let yourself molder under yellowing lights like I did." As he finished talking the record stopped. The needle had completed its course across the dark spinning disk. "Before you go, would you mind taking off that record for me? My hands, they shake more than they used to."

"Certainly." The needle popped as Jody lifted the ancient arm of the machine, and the hiss of the rolling record subsided into still, silence. As if on queue, the chill running back and forth down Jody's spine ceased and the uneasy feeling crawling along his skin left his body. He laid his hands on the record, now sitting in stillness atop the turntable. For the first time, the label of the old record was legible to Jody. The title Stabat Mater was emblazoned across it in white above a stylized picture of a turn of the century orchestra imposed on a black background. Jody picked up the time-worn record from the turntable and returned it to its sleeve.

Mr. Tipton looked up. His eyes caught the faded square in his gaze. He squinted and his lips flattened and thinned, eyes bulged behind his glasses, and the color washed from his face. "It's my favorite, you know." His voice quivered. "Nothing else like it in the world, but I think I've heard enough for now."

"It's a very curious favorite, sir." The lamenting tones of the piece, now familiar to everyone who worked there, seemed more dirge than anything else. Jody didn't understand why anyone would hold it in such high esteem.

"Thank you, Jody. That is all."

CHAPTER
FIVE

J ody pulled his jacket closed tight around his chest with a clinched fist in the brisk spring night air. A gentle mist glistened in the light of the street lamps as he trod up the hill from the car he left parked on the street. The neighborhood of Mt. Adams took its name literally. The narrow streets and steeply inclined hills gave the little community a flavor completely unique amongst all others in Cincinnati. The cold air whipped through the alleys and down the steep streets, and scalded his face as he made his way toward the Blind Lemon.

The old brick building was a welcomed sight indeed. The outdoor lighting poured over the rough brick, warmly illuminating the three striped awnings over the two front windows and the door. Silently, he descended a narrow staircase of uneven hewn stone slabs into a tiny offset alleyway. It felt like he was stepping into an old black and white gangster movie. The brick walls pressed in on him with every step and silently wept with the energy of a century of secrets whispered and rubbed into them by countless feet just as unsure as his own. He opened the door and felt the warmth wash over him, as he glanced at his watch. It was 8:15. A knot grew in his stomach. She would either be there, or she wouldn't.

He made his way through the narrow passages of the unique night spot. The wood and stone interior of the front room was wonderfully decorated. The walls contained everything from carefully encased antique cars and trains to metal pots. The seats in the serving area were placed close together, the room so narrow it more closely resembled a hallway than a serving floor. Nearly each seat was filled with people sipping coffees and drinks, laughing and making merry. Jody pressed on past the small fireplace and down the hallway to the back room where Rodger would be playing.

He carefully navigated past a particularly boisterous gentleman, gesticulating so wildly with his arms, Jody had to nearly belly up to the wall to pass by. He moved deftly beyond the man's reach and crossed over to the opposite end of the double-faced fireplace. The decor continued with antique portraits hanging along with golden records. He laid his eyes on the most attractive sight of all, Meg, seated at a table for two opposite the ornate wooden bar. He sat down across from her and breathed a sigh of relief.

"Is this guy good or what?" she asked sipping from her brown bottle. She sat it back down on the table and Jody watched a single drop of condensation fall from the glass neck, down and across the label that read "Chistian Morlein."

"He's good." Jody replied. "Not as good as the original, but he's pretty good."

"Can I buy you a drink?" Meg offered.

"No thanks. You know I don't drink."

"Oh, yes, that's right. You're a tea-totaler. Well how about a coffee then?"

"Sure, why not."

Meg returned with a coffee, just the way Jody liked it. "I hear you're going home for the summer again."

"Yes, home sweet home." Jody took a sip from his warm, sweet brew. "My parents should be home by then."

"I wish I vacationed as much as your mom and dad." Meg took another drink from her cold beer, never lifting her eyes from the band diligently plying their trade nearby.

"Me too." Jody smiled. "Sometimes I feel like an afterthought; the little puppy at home they have to check in on and feed."

"So, next Monday is it?"

"Yeah, provided I graduate." Jody smirked.

"Very funny. You've made the grade this year just like all the rest of us."

"I guess." Jody pulled a folded piece of paper and handed it to Meg.

She unfolded it. "Three A's, one B, looks like passing grades to me." She handed back the deeply creased paper. "This calls for a celebration." She raised her bottle as he raised his coffee mug. "To Mr. Jody Howard, most recent graduate of the University of Cincinnati School of Business."

Jody responded with a heartfelt tip of his mug and another drink of his warm brew. The celebratory sip of warm coffee seemed all the more satisfying, not because it was taken in commemoration of his academic accomplishment, but because it was taken with Meg.

He spent a few quiet moments across from her, silently drinking in her subtle mannerisms as he sipped coffee. She leaned slightly over the table toward him, her elbow resting on the table and her legs crossed beneath it. The slender, brown forearm rose straight and true from the polished wooden platform like a dark obelisk, crowned by her perfectly curved face, cradled, cheek in hand. Her eyelashes batted softly. Darkened by mascara, they perfectly framed her lovely deep eyes; eyes that seemed to look past him. She was watching Rodger as he played in the corner.

Her fingers were tipped with red polish that only served to accent her dark complexion and perfect skin. Ruby tipped fingers fell back gently to the table and resumed tracing the outline of her cold, sweating bottle. "Roger! Good to see you."

"And you," Roger spoke from just behind Jody's head jolting his mind open to the rest of the surrounding world. "How are the two of you doing tonight?"

"Oh, I'm just fine. Thanks for asking," Meg offered her hand to be gently embraced by him in a friendly handshake.

"Me too, just fine." Jody cleared his throat.

He hadn't even noticed the music had stopped. How fortunate that his friend, from their hallowed alma mater's hall of Mary Emery, had paid his table a visit just in time to shine the cold light of truth on his great and forlorn hope.

"Well thanks for coming tonight to hear us. Hey, I've got to go get back, but it sure is nice to see you again."

"Thanks," Meg and Jody said in unison.

"Jinx," Jody taunted in a half-hearted wish of true ill will, not directed toward Meg but to the mighty and indefatigable Roger.

"No, you can't call jinx on that."

"Yes, yes I did, and I win." Jody laughed uncomfortably, shifting heavily in his seat. The weight of the warm mug in his hand increased as he lifted it to his parched lips.

Meg sighed and sank back in her chair as Rodger's band began to play. "Just look at that man sing." She said all she needed to say.

Jody turned and watched the band as they rolled seamlessly into their next song. Warm tones flowed out of the house sound system like slow moving honey from a waterspout. Jody lost himself in his friend's show, choosing to let go of the here and now and allow their sounds to salve the festering wounds hidden so deeply inside his soul. He didn't dare touch them on his own. A glisten grew in his eye as tears welled up inside, and the band played on before him, around him, within him.

Roger's velvety voice called out the next song. "This next one is called Dust My Broom by the legend B. B. King."

Jody smiled and nodded his head to the rhythm as Rodger closed his steely eyes and crooned out the old tune with enough soul to make the King himself proud. Jody rode the soulful wave, commiserating and rejoicing with the lyrics all at the same time. The room roared with applause when the band finished. He couldn't hold a grudge, not when a maestro like Roger took the mic and worked the room. Roger never failed to move him deeply from whatever stage he took, large or small.

"Wow, that was hot," Meg strained into Jody's ear over raucous applause echoing through the cramped room.

"You're tellin' me..." Jody clapped and smiled at Meg.

He fell in love with her just a little in that moment, not just a desire, not just a curiosity, but an infinitesimal ember of genuine and passionate adoration. It flickered and was snuffed to ashes in the same instant, as the realization that none of the light in her cheeks or sparkle in her eyes was due to any other than the great maestro himself, Roger. Jody repaired his broken heart with another warm sip of coffee as Meg shouted Roger's name.

The hometown band answered the adoring crowd by laying down an unbelievably smooth version of "Like A Rolling Stone" by Bob Dylan. Jody couldn't believe his ears and couldn't stop smiling and crying at the same time, proud of his friend, and hurt for himself.

The crowd voiced their approval once more after the last note was played. "Thank you all. You're so very kind. Thank you," Rodger wiped a few beads of sweat from his brow with his sleeve. "I'm going to switch it up just a moment and play a song for a friend here with us from Virginia for what might be the last time. He's all grown up now and going home with a ticket for success from the dean and board of regents of the University of Cincinnati. Cheers Jody, and you too Meg."

He cleared his throat, turned to the band and counted off the next song. His comfortable, Kentucky accent slipped silkily through his lips like a mountain spring. The first line of "The Night They Drove Old Dixie Down" poured from his lips. Rodger let each verse rise and fall, expressing emotion so pure, so sincere, that it nearly made Jody miss home, not his real home here in Cincinnati, the empty one in the lonely Virginia hills.

Masterfully executed chord progression and lamenting lyrics carried him away. The sad words and message of forlorn hope somehow allowed him a small window of respite to remember good things from his childhood and growing up; his friends, his family, and the loving touch of his father's hand on his shoulder as they fished in the river together.

He heard his father's deep velvet voice, "Remember Jody, I am always going to be here for you, always."

Jody hated shows of emotion, but he just couldn't seem to help it tonight. He found himself tearing up a bit again, not from his petty girl problems, but from the feeling of utter security that came with that memory; knowing his dad was there, believing he always would be.

Then, the security shattered. "I want you. She hates you." A dark snakelike voice slithered around his brain.

"Look at you, all grown up; from Hill Billy to City Dweller." Meg said tipping her bottle in his direction.

Jody felt something different. Anger. It reared up inside as quickly as the unwanted voice that tormented him. He rolled his eyes and scoffed. If there was one thing that sat him on edge, it was being called a Hill Billy, especially by pontificating urbanites who had never stooped below their station to live south of the Ohio river.

"You know not everyone born south of the Mason-Dixon line is raised up barefoot and bigoted."

"I know. Not *everyone*." Meg jabbed.

"Not even..." Jody stopped mid-sentence checking the fiery ball that was building deep in the pit of his stomach. He loved to argue almost as much as Meg loved goading him. "No, no. You know what? You are not going to get me started tonight." He laughed.

"Oh, come on." Meg smiled pawing at the air with her perfectly manicured hands. "You are so cute when you get all upset. Your cheeks get puffy, and those nostrils flare out."

"You are pretentious and manipulative." He smiled, pointing a finger toward her rosy cheeks. "And I am not playing your little game. Tonight, I live."

"You're so funny when you drink too much. Bar tender, this man needs to be cut off," she said in a raised voice. "He has had far too much caffeine to drink tonight."

"Ha, ha very funny."

Meg giggled uncontrollably. Jody smiled. He loved that sound, the sound of her being happy. That was his favorite sound in the world. It made him forget his anger.

"Oh, you kill me, Jody." She gently patted his hand, each small touch sent electricity sparking up his arm almost causing him to twitch.

"You're wonderful." Jody blurted. The words seemed to tumble out of his mouth like a drunken sailor off the poop deck. Meg looked at him, unchanged, like a marble statue; not cold, full of beauty, but unsettlingly unchanged by events transpiring around her. Jody lectured himself inside his head about his stupid choice of words and his horrible timing.

"Just look at the way he handles that guitar." Meg observed over Jody's shoulder. "Like he's slow dancing with it."

Jody choked on his last sip of coffee, nearly spitting it on his lap. "At least he can't step on its toes."

The moment was over. He tried to recover some of his lost pride with an awkward joke. He wished she hadn't said that. He had hoped she wanted to meet him tonight. Instead, Roger had all of her attention without even saying a word. He didn't turn to watch him swaying with the old, weathered Martin. He knew it was true. Roger was confident, suave, and had perfect pitch; all admirable qualities that he couldn't even begin to emulate, much less compete with.

Mercifully, Meg's phone began to ring in her purse. She fumbled trying to find it until it fell out onto the table. "Hello," she brushed a small tendril of hair from her eyes. "Hello?" The sound of squelching screaming static on the other line, so loud even Jody could hear it. Her eyes widened, one last hello and she smashed the red button on the screen and slammed the phone face down on the table. "Okay... that was weird."

Jody nodded knowingly, eyebrows raised. He lifted the mug up once more, but this time was disappointed when there was not enough delicious brew remaining to wet his lips. He stared at the bottom of the mug when Meg pushed her chair noisily away from the table.

"How could you!?" She stared daggers into his shocked wide eyes. "Why would you say that?"

"What are you talking about?"

She stormed past him and out the door without so much as another word. Everything stopped for a moment. After she disappeared into the tiny hallway headed toward the street above, the band began again and conversations resumed in spits and spurts.

Jody toyed with the dying foam of whipped cream clinging the bottom of his mug. "That was a fitting end to an evening of disappointment." He sat the mug down quietly and continued to listen for some time, contemplating his confusion and shame in the solitude of his table for one.

"Can I get you anything else?" The young, blonde waitress asked looking down at him behind smiling cheeks.

"Did you hear...." He stopped. He knew she hadn't, even if she had, how would he ever be able to describe what was going on in his anxious thoughts?

"Please?"

"Never mind." He smiled back. "I'm ready for the check."

CHAPTER
SIX

His car door closed behind him in the still empty parking garage, echoing off the cement pillar. The cacophonous, lonely sound confirmed the end of an ordeal he did not wish to ever repeat. Bravely, he had stepped forth into the Cincinnati night life and dipped his toe into the mysterious pool of the feminine mystique. What he had hoped to be a first date with Meg had turned into a Roger love fest. He had spent most of Sunday sulking in front of the television, wondering if Meg had finally sealed the deal with her heartthrob. Now, Monday was upon him and he could only hope and pray it would be merciful.

The walk to The Study Hall was dark and cool. A slight dampness hovered in the air from a gentle rain that had fallen the night before. He had taken this stroll hundreds of times, but this time was different. This morning his footsteps seemed to resonate in the silence. He wasn't used to being so alone in the city. There was no hustle or bustle, only him and the sound of his sneakers pounding on the damp pavement like a marching army, reverberating off of the stony facades.

Step by step he came closer to the old brick storefront. His steps slowed. He shivered and stopped. It was as if a cold breeze had flowed across his chest and arms, every hair stood on end, but there was nothing. No wind blew, not even a wisp of air in motion around the storefront.

Jody waited, every sense acute, every nerve on edge. His eyes scanned up, down, left and right but his head stood perfectly still. His ears rang in the stillness, as if a giant speaker system was feeding back in his head. Every inch of skin crawled with electricity. Someone was watching him. They had to be. He snapped his head to look back over his shoulder. Nothing.

He took in a long, deep breath to reset his senses and looked inside the store window. The shop was dimly lit by a single lamp in the back corner. A thin shaft of warm light crawled across the room from beneath the closed door to the back.

A loud, screeching, mournful noise broke the silence. Every synapse in his brain fired at once, every muscle jerked to life and filled with adrenaline. His heart pounded and his stomach leapt up into his throat. He gave out a quivering half scream. "Ahh-hh!" but he stopped himself, choking back the sound. It was only a car squealing its tires as it sped through the intersection behind him. The engine revved and faded as it continued on its way down the dark streets.

Jody cleared his throat as he checked his pockets one more time, hoping the ritual would help him pull his emotions together.

"Coffee," he muttered to himself.

He pulled the lump of keys from his right front pants pocket and fumbled with it. The cold metal of the worn and tarnished key slid into the lock and turned until he heard the click of the tumblers sliding open. .

The wet soles of his sneakers squeaked across the welcome mat as he closed the door behind him. "Good morning Mr. Tipton," he called out.

He gently rubbed his eyes and looked at the counter, resolute in purpose. "Coffee," he mumbled to himself again.

The only thing that could clear his mind of the cobwebs was a good jolt of java in a nice warm cup. The loudly whirring mechanism inside the stainless-steel machine ground some beans into coarse grinds. Jody poured fresh water into the machine and began brewing the first pot of coffee for the day.

The machine began to percolate with a familiar clatter. Warm aromas wafted silently into Jody's nose. The day was turning better already. He became more aware of his surroundings as he waited on his drink to brew. He turned on the main lights. The fluorescent bulbs above him flickered and their light built into a radiant blue wash that caused his corneas to burn.

He blinked until the room once again came into focus. The gurgling crescendo behind him told of the good news. His coffee was done. He poured himself a long-anticipated mug and sipped with satisfaction.

As his taste buds danced, Jody took in the room. Something was amiss, not something big, something very small. It was so small that he had to carefully look for three or four minutes before his conscious mind put the pieces together. There, on the center table of the room, sat three books laying at angles, one of them opened as if someone had been reading and only just stepped away.

"That's odd," Jody reflected as he walked over. He sat his coffee down on the table and examined the books. The one on the left was immediately recognizable. Its worn yellow cover and red lettering gave it away as it sat closed and face up. He didn't even have to read the title "Dracula." The other closed book lay on the right. It was more nondescript; a brown leather cover with black lettering. The book in the center was opened almost to the middle and looked welcoming enough. Jody placed his hands on the pages and turned to the title page. "The False Faces by Louis Joseph Vance", it read, and on the bottom of the page was the date 1918.

Jody thought perhaps Mr. Tipton had gotten them out to

read them after he got in this morning. He lifted his mug to take another sip of coffee, facing the backroom door. Then, his ears opened and became aware of a gentle rhythmic sound coming from behind the door. It was scratchy and gravelly. He had heard that sound before, but where and when? His mind searched. Rhythmic, gentle, the sound was so soft it previously escaped his perception. It was the skipping of the old record player, repeating that same cadence over and over because the needle was off track.

"Good morning Mr. Tipton," Jody projected, hoping to see his boss scoot through the doorway at any moment. He did not, and Jody's heart began to race.

Jody approached the hidden doorway along the back wall. He touched the cold knob and paused. Who was behind the door? His heart beat faster as he took a deep breath. "Mr. Tipton," he called again with more urgency.

Thoughts and scenarios rushed through Jody's mind. Maybe the old man was in the bathroom and didn't want to be bothered. Maybe it's not him at all. Maybe it's some kind of a book-loving thief. After all, wouldn't it make sense for a book lover to rob an antique bookstore? Whoever it was, now knew Jody was there, and knew Jody was just on the other side of the door. The thing behind the door could not be ignored. Retreat into the deserted streets was not a safe option.

Jody braced himself, muscles tight and ready to spring, then flung the door open as fast and hard as he possibly could. He invaded the closure of the back room with a throaty grunt. Then, only stillness, nothing happened. There was no reaction, verbal or physical, to his intrusion.

He turned to look at the record player. Beside the gently undulating needle and turntable was Mr. Tipton, slumped in his chair with his head resting on his right shoulder. His mouth was open, tongue protruding gently through his lips. He looked as if he were snoring, but his skin was pale, his body still and perfectly motionless.

Jody rushed to his side. "Mr. Tipton! Can you hear me Mr. Tipton?" But the old man's bones made no reply. Jody touched his hand and his face. They were cold as ice. Jody stumbled back and fell groping for the wooden floor behind him. He cried out in fear and sadness. His emotions whirled inside of his chest like a maelstrom.

Jody rose, hot tears streaming down his face and picked up the black phone from Mr. Tipton's desk and dialed 9-1-1. When the operator answered, Jody's words got caught in his throat and began to choke him. He couldn't look at the cold dead body of the man he had grown to care so much about and still speak. He had to turn his back on the corpse before he was finally able to cough out the words. Jody sank to the floor and waited until help came.

The whole world flew by like a blurry movie all around him. Someone in a dark uniform helped him into the front room and sat him down, but he didn't know by whom or exactly how long ago.

"Jody, Jody," a female voice faded in and out. "Jody, can you hear me?" It became clearer, and Jody's mind focused. The world stopped spinning. It was daylight outside. Meg sat across the table from him. "Jody, can you hear me?"

He shook his head in slow reply.

"Are you ok? What happened?"

"Excuse me, Mr. Howard," a strong male voice called out from above him. "I know that this is a difficult time, but I'm going to need to ask you a few questions." Jody looked up at the officer. He was dressed in a crisp black police uniform. Jody shook his head yes as the tall officer's partner ushered Meg away so they could speak more privately. The conversation was difficult, and Jody had to concentrate hard on each question.

When it was finally over, the officer thanked him, and he beckoned Meg to sit back in the chair beside him.

Gentle fingers rubbed tiny circles across his back. Meg's quiet voice spoke to him in a slow and reassuring rhythm. He couldn't really comprehend what she was saying, but it didn't matter. Her touch brought some comfort, but he was still confused, unable to get his bearings as the world spun around him. He was adrift and empty. The last man alive he could truly look up to was gone forever.

"I'm... I'm sorry... I didn't... I... I..."

"It's okay. It's okay. It's not important now." Meg drew him closer to her in a genuine embrace. "How did he die?"

CHAPTER
SEVEN

"It was like it was happening all over again." Jody spoke into a black cordless phone tucked up between his cheek and his shoulder.

"I don't know I... I just fell apart, I guess. I don't remember much." He could partially see down the narrow hallway from where he sat at his small wooden table in the dining area of his apartment. On the hallway wall he looked blankly at his family photo from his sophomore year of high school.

"No, no," he shook his head, "I didn't, no, he was already," choking on his words "already gone when I got there." He took his fork and played with a mangled lump of cooling macaroni and cheese sitting on his plate.

"Not yet, but we should know something soon. It's been more than a day already."

Each face in the photo was etched into his brain, every expression, every stitch of clothing. It didn't matter that he couldn't plainly see it from his vantage point. He knew exactly what story it told.

"I've been just relaxing, you know, collecting my thoughts, I guess. Huh? Oh, no, no one has been in there since, at least not that I know of."

He closed his eyes preferring to look at the picture as he remembered it, rather than strain to make out the details from his chair.

"I'm fine. I'm fine. No, don't please. I...I want you to enjoy yourself." Jody chuckled softly, trying to sound as if it were possible for his heart to feel light.

"Sure, bring me back something with one of those Inca pyramids on it. Mayan pyramids ok, sorry. Sure, uh huh, ok, yes, I love you too, mom."

The line clicked. Silence filled his tiny apartment. It sat suspended, heavy in the air like so much gray smoke; palpable, real, and offensive to the senses. The silence spoke of a heaviness, a longing inside, not so much from the passing of Mr. Tipton, but for something he had lost a long time ago on that fateful trip with his father.

Jody sat the phone down on the table beside his plate. He lifted a bite of yellow, gooey macaroni and cheese to his mouth. It sat on his tongue and tasted well enough, but he could not chew it. He had lost his appetite, for both food and silence. Jody let his fork fall to his plate with a rattling clang, scooted his chair away from the table and walked over to his blue suede couch. He reached for his remote control, so he could ruminate in front of the droning television.

The technicolor faces on the tv screen fazed in and out of frame without Jody taking note of any of them. One after another, the faces suddenly appeared and then melted away. Blankly, he looked straight ahead, allowing the flashes of color and onslaught of sounds numb him to reality.

There was order to a television program, a purpose reflecting all the colors of life. His life seemed to lack purpose, lack direction. There was no real enemy to defeat, no great disaster to prevent, no life lesson to teach a younger generation. There was only him, only the now, a present reality in which he no longer wished to be a participant.

As another set of credits scrolled up the television screen, Jody became aware. It was night. He pulled open the blinds and looked out over his tiny balcony. Jody stepped through, into the night. The stars were out. It wasn't often that he got to see stars from his deck, surrounded by the urban sprawl. It was a welcomed sight. He panned the horizon looking for familiar shapes, the constellations he had learned as a child, but his view of the sky was far too limited, and he couldn't make sense out of the flickering balls of light.

On dark twinkling nights like this, his father loved to take the family camping. They would pick the perfect site out in the woods to set up a tent. He remembered the smell of dingy plastic and the way his father would raise a hammer to drive in each tent stake, and then cap off the raising of the tent by declaring, "There we go. It'll be a great place to sleep tonight provided it doesn't fall in on us."

They would all lie on blanket where they could see the stars and would talk and laugh. He would listen to his father explain the constellations. Each one was simple but radiant, each one now unforgettable. Maybe someday he would have a son to teach how to touch stars with his fingertips and tell beautiful stories to in the night.

It was Father's Day when he and his dad went on a special trip together. They had set their tent near the Red River, deep in the Gorge in the Daniel Boone National Forrest, and fished out on the water all day long. He loved time with his dad, and that day the only thing that disrupted their time together was the occasional nibble on the line. That night they lay out on the bank and the black velvet sky was wider and more brilliant than he had ever seen in his life, before or since. They talked for the entire night.

Jody remembered his father's voice. It played over and over again in his head. He had committed large portions of their conversation that night to memory.

As he thought on his father's words, he reconstructed his father's warm features in his mind's eye. Those features used to bring him such joy, but tonight they were covered with a thin veil of palled skin, milky, cold, just like Mr. Tipton's skin the night...

"No!" he screamed, into the inky sky.

He closed the sliding glass door behind him and locked it. The shades were returned to their normal positions, ready to blot out the sun as best they could the next morning. He turned off the television and walked down the dimly lit hallway, pausing to look at the family picture one last time for the night. He studied his father's features closely and tried to return the color into his father's face. That picture was taken just a week before the trip. It was a portrait of his family, exactly as he wanted to remember it.

The gurgling ring of his telephone pierced the silence before he reached his bedroom. Jody walked in and threw himself face down on the bed and reached over to the nightstand to grab the phone.

"Hello."

"Hi Jody." It was Meg. "So, how have you been?"

If there had ever been such a pointed and hard-hitting question Jody had not heard it. Who was she to ask such a personal question, and right off the bat without any social niceties? He could not bring himself to open up, to give her the real answer, not that she would even want to hear it. So, he lied. "I'm doing ok."

"Anything on your mind," she persisted.

He knew there was no way she was that clueless. Of course, there was something on his mind. "No," he lied again.

"Don't be obtuse, Jody. I know he's on your mind." Her words were met with silence. "I wish I could reach through this phone and..."

"Slap me?" Jody stood up and started pacing around the

room. He didn't want another awkward phone conversation tonight.

"No, hug you." Her voice cracked and Jody could hear the faintest sniffle on the other end of the phone. "I wish I could hug you, Jody, and pull you out of this funk."

The sadness in Meg's voice pulled emotions buried deep inside of Jody to the surface. A tear fell halfway down his cheek and he quickly wiped it away with his sleeve. He wanted that too, but he was sure she didn't want it for all the same reasons. Sure, he wanted comfort, but he wanted, he needed companionship, and that was something she clearly wasn't willing to provide.

Meg cleared her throat and tried to soldier on through the conversation. "The coroner's report has finally come out. Have you heard about it yet?"

"I haven't."

"They determined the cause of death to be a heart attack, and he probably passed away sometime Sunday night."

Jody got a sick feeling in his stomach and his skin began to crawl. Mr. Tipton had sat there all night. He didn't want to think about it. It was both heart breaking and disgusting.

"Ok, thanks. Thanks for letting me know."

"Look, Jody, I know that what you went through, what you've been through, is horrible. I can't imagine what that feels like. I just want you to know that it's not your fault."

"I know it's not my fault. Don't be ridiculous."

"That's not what I'm talking about." She waited on him to offer an acknowledgement that never came. "It happened again last night."

"What happened?"

"You know what, Jody. I was there, remember." If she could have physically forced him to talk about it she would have. "You saw Mr. Tipton's body, and…". She didn't want to have to say it herself. "…It happened again."

"Meg, I..."

She had enough of the delicate tiptoeing. "Say it, Jody." The subject had to be breached. No matter what.

"No..."

"Say it! Four letters, Jody, just say it."

An agonizing groan went from Jody's lips over the telephone. "I don't..."

"Fine let me say it for you." She spelled it out for him, letter by letter. "P-T-S-D."

Jody cried out loud and crumpled to the ground, his back leaning heavily against the wall. "No, I don't... I don't want to. I can't..."

"Jody, listen to me. Say it... You have to say it."

He sobbed. He didn't want to say its name, that monster that had followed him from Kentucky, to Virginia, and even across the river to the University of Cincinnati. To say its name was to give it power, to admit that he was powerless. "I don't want to."

"You're never going to heal, you're never going to beat this, until you're ready to face it. Stop running away, just say it."

"PTSD". The words vomited from his mouth and raked his throat. "P-T-S-D."

"Remember what you told me earlier? You said your therapist had you on step three. What was that again? Re... re...". She couldn't connect the dots in her mind.

"Reconnection and integration."

"Yeah, you have to look ahead to the future, to find a new voice for yourself. Did you ever call your therapist back like you said you would?"

"No."

Meg mustered as much compassion and care into her voice as she possibly could. "Come on Jody, you can do this. Call him, please. You've come so far. You can finish this. You can feel normal again. You just need to, you know, release your feelings, allow yourself to grieve."

Jody felt indignant. "I need to allow myself to grieve? I am grieving, Meg. This is how I grieve, ok. I don't need you calling me up at night reminding me how to grieve."

Meg raised her voice to match his. "You are not grieving. You're hiding in your shell. You can't just shut yourself off from the world and call it the blues. I know what the blues are, Jody Howard. The blues are crying yourself to sleep, eating too much rocky road ice cream and asking friends to help shove chocolate down your throat while you tell them all about your problems. That is the blues. Not hiding in a hole somewhere and pretending that you are ok."

"I am trying to..."

"No, you are not." Meg quickly lowered her voice. "You are trying to pretend that nothing happened so you can bottle it all up inside and have it fester in you for years just like..."

This time Jody cut her off. "Don't you go there. Do not even go there, Meg," he growled. "You didn't sit there with him, Meg. You didn't touch him. You didn't sit there waiting for hours with him bleeding all over you, cold and bleeding." Jody trailed off and tried not to sob. He didn't want her to hear him cry, but he was panicking, his breaths fast and shallow, his arms and hands shaking uncontrollably. He was there again, just like seven years ago, trapped alone and unable to escape.

Meg was silent. Jody choked on his tears on his end of the phone. This wasn't about Mr. Tipton. It was about his dad.

"Look um, um," she stammered, "I'm sorry. I, I didn't mean to bring that up."

"It's ok, Meg." his voice quivered and cracked.

They each sat there still on the phone for a while, consumed in the sound of the other's breathing, trying to imagine what the other was thinking.

"I heard Mr. Tipton's lawyer stopped by last night," Meg finally spoke up.

"Yeah, its mine now." Jody's eyes rolled back into his head. "I don't know what I'm doing, but its mine."

"I don't believe that. You know what you're doing. You've trained for years for this."

"I don't know, Meg. I'd just rather..."

"Have faith...just a little faith...in yourself. It's going to be fine."

Faith was a hollow word. It meant nothing to Jody. Any real fortitude he had left, any belief in something better, something bigger than himself, died on the floor beside Mr. Tipton.

"Meg, I can't talk anymore. I need to...."

"I need you to open the store." Her words were quick and impatient. Jody could hear her breathing speed up on the other end of the phone as she awaited his response. "I need you to not give up. I need... we need you to open the store again."

"Meg, I..."

A few days ago, he had no real prospects. His only option was to go back to an empty home in Virginia and serve as his mother and stepfather's house sitter as they gallivanted all over the world. It was depressing. Now, he had his opportunity handed to him; an entire business, already standing, in an industry he was familiar with, with a staff he had known for years, just given to him on a silver platter by the creepy old man in the dusty hidden back room.

"If you don't agree, then I am coming to your apartment tomorrow and I am bringing Billy with me." The ultimatum had been laid down.

Jody threw his back against the wall and slowly slid to the floor. "Oh, come on, Meg."

The store now represented something to Jody, even more intimidating than the creepy feeling he would get amongst the aging stacks of books on long nights. It was a vision and a future where there had been none. It was his to grasp, to hold, to nurture and love into tomorrow. It held so much promise, but it also held real risk. No one would expect success when there were no real prospects. Struggles, hardship, failure, would all be expected. But now, he was being handed a living, breathing business. Mr. Tipton had carefully fashioned it into a success. Jody feared failure. If he failed in Virginia, no one would know but his absentee family. If he failed here, at the Study Hall, then his friends, his whole community would feel it, would see it burn to the ground before their very eyes, with him at the helm.

"Open the store up tomorrow, or Billy Johnston is chillin' at your place all afternoon. What do you say?"

"That's insane!"

His stomach turned and he nearly retched at the very thought. He would have sole responsibility; budgets, invoices, procurement, schedules, repairs, payroll, benefits. The list of challenges went on and on. He wanted to try. He wanted to do it; if for no other reason than to not let down Meg, and to not let down Billy. He might succeed. It was always possible that he could do the right thing and not let the whole enterprise burn down around him.

"Rip the band aid off! Get it over with. Otherwise..." Her voice trailed off for a second before she cleared her throat and regained her composure. "Otherwise, you'll just never do it and it'll all be over. I'm not ready for it to all be over, Jody. Are you?"

EIGHT

The familiar brass bell above the door called out, welcoming Jody home to his store for the first time. Personal ownership was a concept so foreign to Jody he had to repeat the phrase a couple of times to even walk all the way in through the doorway.

"My store."

He had met with the attorney, signed all the papers, and was handed a metal key. It felt small and cold in his hand, but heavy with responsibility. It was, in every way as he could tell, exactly like the key he was given by Mr. Tipton so many years ago, but this one was different. It was the master key. From it sprang all access, all copies, all permissions, all responsibilities, and that master key was now his, alone.

As he entered, his footsteps echoed off the walls. It felt very empty, a vast chasm of nothingness disguised behind a facade of bookshelves and coffee fare. The room was cold, devoid of life, and shadowy.

He slung his jacket up over the back of a wooden chair. Jody never lowered his eyes. He kept them up, still scanning the room for something he felt was there, hovering just outside his vision. A strange feeling of nameless loss returned.

"This is creepy."

Emptiness consumed him and contorted his perceptions. Shadows flicked and flitted across the room as passing cars sent glinting reflections of light through the windows.

Jody turned on every light in the shop from front to back in an attempt to vanquish the uneasiness that had settled over him. He stepped quietly behind the coffee bar and began brewing himself a fresh pot, just like he had done the last time he had been in the room. A rich, decadent aroma filled the air. He breathed deep and filled his body with the scent of fresh, hand-picked, roasted coffee beans.

He sipped his first cup of Highlander Grog and immediately his nerves began to calm. Cup in hand, he strolled over to the bookshelves and casually perused the titles, allowing his eyes to enjoy the different sizes, shapes, colors, and conditions of each spine.

"Okay, this is more like it."

He entered the back room. The door creaked and his foot haltingly crossed the threshold. Emotional tension boiled up deep inside his core and caused his stomach to rumble. The room was a bit more disheveled than usual, but that was to be expected. His desk looked just as he had left it. The same filing cabinets still stood stoically against the wall, and there, in the same corner, the stack of books he so loathed.

"I will get you yet," he scolded the pile as it slunk there silently in contempt.

"No, you won't," the snake hissed in his head.

"Shut up!" Jody's scream echoed off the aging walls. His lips quivered and he groaned, rubbing his face with his hands in frustration. "Focus," he whispered to himself. "just stay on task."

Mr. Tipton's old desk sat stoically in the same place it had for more than three decades, his lonely, weathered chair behind it. Jody cringed, and stretched out his hand allowing his fingers to gently dance across the surface of the desk. He was forcing himself to touch it, teaching himself that there was nothing inherently wrong with the object.

"Just another old desk."

Jody grabbed the back of Mr. Tipton's leather chair and pulled it out. He tried to sit, but he couldn't. The memory of Mr. Tipton's cold body slumped over in the chair haunted him. His hair stood on end and his nerves tingled at the very thought of sitting where the dead man sat for hours. He couldn't do it. The wheels underneath the steel legs squealed across the floor as Jody pulled it over to his old desk and brought back his own, more familiar, chair instead.

The aging computer whirred and groaned to life. Jody began delicately sifting through loose papers and receipts categorizing them after his own fashion. He had only just begun to make his mark on the business; a gentle reorganization, a bit timid at first, as if he were a curator cleaning a display late at night in the Smithsonian.

He chuckled to himself, "I'm running a business, not a museum."

Jody poured over the numbers and documents that made The Study Hall run behind the scenes. He studied every paragraph and every budget line item. It was exhausting work.

Time had slipped away from him. The old grandfather clock in the front room began to gong and toll out the ninth hour. Jody looked up from his work and noticed his empty coffee mug.

"Another cup?"

He took tender steps on stiffened legs into the front room. His muscles ached from atrophy. He thought on the pain and how it must have been so familiar to Mr. Tipton. Jody knew this newfound career would require much more sitting and reckoning than moving about. The sedentary lifestyle that lay ahead terrified him. He remembered Mr. Tipton's warnings and musings. They brought a chill to his spine and a realization that he could not hide in his little back room cocoon forever.

He let his mind wander and swim freely in the beautiful golden lamp light as he refilled his mug. "Is it worth it; hours and hours in this aging place?" He answered after taking a sip, "not as if it would be *that* big of a change for me. I already spend most of my free time here."

He drew a sense of resoluteness up within himself as he slowly sipped and contemplated. Maybe, just maybe, this could be his shot. He wanted certainty and happiness. This place could finally bring that to him, or at least perhaps it could. He would have purpose.

"Maybe I would."

The warm, mouthwatering brew slipped down his throat, leaving behind just a hint of sweetness and aftertaste on his tongue. He relished it; the taste of warm coffee mingled with newfound responsibility. He felt alive.

"It's mine. I'm keeping it," he announced to the empty room, declaring lordship over his realm of coffee and printed words bound in leather and crackling paper covers. "The Study Hall will open for business again Saturday morning. Too much down time is bad for business."

He grabbed a napkin from the dispenser at the coffee bar and wiped the drop of coffee that was running down the side of his mug and then dabbed at the corners of his mouth. He meandered into the backroom lost in thought and contemplation. The crumpled and stained napkin flew from his hand into the waste basket beside his new desk. As he watched it leave his hand and arc gently into the trash, he saw something odd that had been discarded in the bin. It was flat and square, a bit oversized for its receptacle. He recognized it, the faded purple and well-worn cover of a record. It was the record Mr. Tipton loved and played every day.

"Hmm, odd." Jody reached in and plucked the old recording

out of the refuse. "I never knew Mr. Tipton to throw anything away." He gently wiped it off on both sides to make sure it was clean.

The great dark square was spun slowly and carefully in his fingers as he examined it. It was thicker than most record sleeves and had some heft about it. "Maybe it fell in here," he posited, but no sooner had he spoken the words than he noticed the impossibility of such a natural occurrence. The stack of records was on the opposite side of the desk. "No, it was tossed," he observed. "I wonder why."

Jody felt it bend and give way in his hands. It was made of two distinct parts bound together like a book. Each half contained a record. He opened it. The inside was not as worn as the outside of the cover. It revealed the work preserved on the vinyl discs. The bold letters running at the top across both pages read "STABAT MATER Opus 58 Antonin Dvorak." Below the title, written in columns running down either panel, were the titles of the ten movements; six on the left, and four on the right, each followed by a respective description.

He had never sat down to hear the entire opus in all of its glory. "I guess I have time now."

Jody took the record over to the record player, removed the first record and placed it on the turntable. The needle gently glided over the familiar grooves as the speakers began to ring forth a beautiful and moving orchestral intro then accompanied by the sound of undulating voices. It was a sorrowful masterpiece, emotion poured out of every note and Jody was captivated by the mesmerizing and colorful world painted by the flowing rhythms and melodies.

The ebb and flow of emotions coming through the antique speakers reminded Jody of the ever-changing tide that filled his own soul. His feelings about his dad, his new family, Mr. Tipton, even his daily struggles seemed to float up to the shore of his experiential consciousness like tangled strands of seaweed.

He closed his eyes and sipped at his coffee as he turned and walked back into the front room. The music echoed in the large empty rooms like a symphony hall. He swayed across the floor and back into the coffee shop carefully holding his cup so as to not spill, while he danced a mournful waltz with an invisible partner.

Once again, the warm brew was raised to his lips and he took in the dark taste and aroma, and then stopped. He stood perfectly still, coffee still touching his lips but not drinking, afraid to open his eyes. He was startled. He thought he heard the voice of a young child, but not quite a voice. It was loud enough to be heard, but the meaning was indistinguishable. It could not have come from outside. The strange sound echoed off the walls like the music from the old record player.

Carefully, he opened his eyes, half expecting to see some small person scuttle about out of sight. When he opened them, nothing moved. All around was clear golden light and rows of books. He slowly panned his face left to right scanning the wall before him, but nothing was out of place.

Once more he tilted back the cup and drank from it. The voice began again, garbled and incoherent, and then it turned to laughter, whimsical laughter, a child's laughter. It moved down the row of bookshelves in front of him, coming closer and closer. Jody quickly sat his coffee down on the table. He looked about franticly seeing nothing amiss, but the laughter continued. The sound encircled him, as if the laughing child danced around his head.

Unsettled, fear welled up inside of him. Tired eyes dashed here and there hoping to see something, anything that would bear physical evidence of an intruder, someone of flesh and blood. Still, he saw nothing but books and the perfectly preserved golden lit rooms.

The voice echoed and chattered in a way that can only be described as not of this world. Laughter ceased as repetitive vowels and consonants came together in stereo around Jody's head. One by one, they coalesced into words, though Jody could not discern their meaning

"Cujus animam germentem," the disembodied child spoke, "contristatem et dolentem, pertransivit gladius."

The words were alien. They meant nothing to Jody, except for the last one, gladius. He recognized it from somewhere, but he couldn't quite place it. It felt old, ancient, like history verbalized. It was Latin, the word for sword. What was so important about a sword? Jody pondered it, rolling the words over in his mind. Then, he realized, he wasn't repeating the phrase at all, the disembodied voice had never stopped repeating the phrase. "Cujus animam germentem contristatem et dolentem, pertransivit gladius."

Jody covered his ears and ran from the building and onto the sidewalk in the rainy night. Spring raindrops beat down upon him like blows from a gauntlet, each wet drop stinging his skin and soaking his clothes. One, two, then three cars passed in rapid succession as Jody's feet beat out their speedy cadence.

He stopped. The voice had gone. He let his hands fall limp to his side as the rain poured over his slunk shoulders. Behind him, he saw golden light spilling out of the shop, pouring across the darkened sidewalk and street. He had left everything on, the lights, the record player, everything. He didn't care. He looked ahead to the intersection determined to not return, but, as he walked away his mind turned to the books, all the merchandise, everything that Mr. Tipton had worked for all of his life. It was all in that store, that unlocked and inviting store.

He fumbled in his pocket and found the store keys. Mr. Tipton's life work could not be stolen by a thief in the night. Heaving his shoulders around, he spun on his heels and turned back toward the shop, forcing himself against abject fear to retrace each step back to the store's front door.

He held the keys out toward the door and wiped the rain from his eyes and peered through the great storefront windows. For a moment, it all seemed so peaceful, like a beautiful urban postcard. The room radiated quaint warmth. Then, near a bookshelf, his eyes detected some sort of movement, but he could discern no form. It was like a watery mirage flying from one side of the room to another.

Standing just behind the giant pane of painted glass of the storefront window stood a boy, eyes dark and sunken, pale lips upturned in the hint of a knowing smile. Hurriedly, he shoved the old keys into the lock and turned until he heard a solid click. As he pulled the key out again, music from the back of the room rose in a beautiful crescendo. Wild feet flew him back toward the parking garage without so much as a passing glance over his shoulder.

The world blurred and then he crashed, knees buckled, and he began to fall. Hands fumbled and arms outstretched, gripping to the thing that had impeded his flight. It was a body, slender, lighter, much weaker than his own. She gasped and he regained his balance catching her just before her body touched the wet pavement. The face and eyes were unmistakable.

"Karen?"

"Jody? What are you doing here?"

CHAPTER
NINE

Sunlight filtered down through wispy morning clouds and found its way gingerly past the hulking frames of high-rise buildings onto the street below. The rain had gone, but the damp air and smell of wet concrete gave testament to its visit the night before. Meg stood at the doorway of the shop looking into the fully lit building, impatiently pacing from window to window.

"I'm coming, don't worry!" Jody's voice warbled as he ran down the sidewalk as quickly as his legs could carry him.

Meg was unimpressed. "Took you long enough."

Last night was life changing. Either Jody was completely insane, or he had made contact with something from the other side, and he wasn't exactly sure which.

"Yeah, well, long night last night."

"I can see." Meg gave an inquisitive and accusatory look. "Why are all the lights on?"

Jody unlocked the door and they both stepped in.

"Correction, why did you leave everything on?" She gestured flamboyantly around the room with her spindly arms.

"Just because," Jody's eyes darted back and forth looking for things to do. He walked over to the table and grabbed his coffee mug from last night and took it to the sink. "Like I said, I just couldn't handle being here by myself last night."

A sly grin grew across Meg's face, and bright eyes beamed from behind raised eyebrows. "Why are you all pale and skittish? Did you see a ghost or something? I was right, wasn't I?"

"No." The short answer was sharp and strangely insistent. Jody wanted to diffuse this line of questioning as quickly as possible. He did not want a conversation about last night's events under any circumstances. "You've told me over and over again that this place is creepy. Well, turns out, you were right. I was here trying to work alone last night, and my skin just started to crawl I was so creeped out." Lying was never Jody's thing, neither were half-truths. He desperately avoided allowing the word ghost to slip through his lips.

Karen was probably already on her way. She told him after their late-night collision that she wanted to meet her friend over a cup of coffee at the store this morning. He couldn't help but hope. Maybe if she stopped by they could talk again and she'd realize how good of a guy he was.

"She can see. You're a fool." The snake hissed deep inside his brain. Jody could feel it, a lying tongue tickling the inside of his ear. He scratched eratically, wanting to claw it out, to purge it from his thoughts.

"Huh, I can't believe it." Meg's voice trailed off. "What are you doing?" She shook her head and turned away, looking around the room. Something was amiss. She saw his coat hanging on one of the wooden chairs in the center of the room. "Wasn't it cold last night?"

Jody walked over immediately and gathered up the coat, darted across the room and hung it on a wobbly wooden coat tree nearby. "And rainy, lots of rain." He grimaced at his inability to control the words coming out of his mouth.

Meg stopped and perked her ears. A strange electric ticking filtered through the thin walls from the back room. It could have gone unnoticed, but for the rhythm of the undulating needle being slightly out of time with the hollow tick of the pendulum in the old grandfather clock. "What's that sound?"

A chill shot down Jody's spine. "Oh that, it's just the record player. I'll get..."

Before he could finish Meg volunteered. "No, I got it." She hurried to the back room and lifted the old needle arm off of the turn table. "A little music to spice up the mood." She slowly lowered the arm until the needle scratched against the still spinning vinyl and the hauntingly beautiful opus began.

Meg's nose scrunched and her mouth contorted as if she'd bitten an apple too tart for her liking. "This is that same morbid stuff Tipton used to listen to. No wonder you ran out of here with the creeps last night."

Jody was quickly on her heels and hurriedly stretched around her to lift the needle from the record with a resounding scratch. "That'll be enough of that for now, thanks."

"Boo!" Meg laughed at him as he recoiled from fright. "Careful, wouldn't want the boogie man to get ya."

"There's no time for that, Meg." They had fifteen minutes until 6 o'clock brought an onrush of very groggy customers begging, palms outstretched, for their morning java fix, not to mention Karen. He had to make time for Karen.

It took a concerted mad dash on both of their parts to make sure everything was ready for Jody to flip the sign from "closed" to "open" precisely at the toll of the hour, as witnessed by the sounding of the old grandfather clock.

Meg was dutifully filling the first order of the day when her phone began buzzing on the coffee bar countertop where she had absentmindedly left it. The rumbling buzz and bright screen caught Jody's attention. Roger's colorful fedora capped face and name stared back at him from the rattling screen.

"Sorry, I'll get that later." She reached over and silenced the call with the press of a button and shoved it into her back pocket.

"That's fine." Jody smiled and called up the next customer, but it was not fine. Roger was calling Meg, and that could mean only one thing. They had been seeing more of each other since the set back at the Blind Lemon. In that one fleeting moment, Jody understood that he had been placed firmly into the friend zone.

Jody put his apron away and quietly excused himself to the back room, allowing the anonymity of the hidden door to shield him from the piercing stares of strangers and the oblivious smiles from the woman who held his heart.

He sat in the squeaky old chair by Mr. Tipton's desk and allowed his train of thought to wonder wildly this way and that, far away from schoolyard crushes and the pain of feelings unrequited.

Mindlessly, his lips began to stammer and stumble over words. "Cujus animam germentem, contristatem et dolentem, pertransivit gladius." He repeated them, and his eyes opened wide, nearly bulging out of his head.

"No!", he gasped. Fumbling hands snatched the well-worn record sleeve from the pile on the desk. He plunked the heavy cardboard square down on the desk. With outstretched arm he strained and flicked the power switch to the old record player. The Stabat Mater by Dvorac popped and cracked into an ethereal existence, the notes and words hanging heavily in the darkened room like a blue cloud of cigar smoke. Jody listened intently until he found it, the words, enunciated perfectly in chorus.

The old computer on the desk whirred to life. Nimble fingers quickly typed out a Google search for Stabat Mater and he poured over the results. The Stabat Mater was an ancient prayer set to music by many different composers. It was always performed in the original language. It was a Catholic prayer...then Latin, the language must be Latin.

"I know about as much Latin as I do Japanese."

He lay his hand on the faded record cover and raised an eyebrow. "Maybe it has an insert."

His fingers carefully pried apart the empty sleeve. He traced the aged cardstock cover with his fingertip, and it stopped as he reached his epiphany. "Cujus animam germentem contristatem et dolentem, pertransivit gladius," he mouthed silently. "Her spirit cried out, full of anguish and sorrow as if pierce by a sword."

"Her spirit?....Pierced by a sword?" Jody tried hard to pull the puzzle pieces together. "But it's a...boy." The same haunting materialization of the faint grin on the pallid young face that happened in the window the night before replayed in Jody's mind.

"It's a...boy?"

He pushed away from the desk and paced. Unable to clear his head and put the puzzle pieces in his mind together neatly, he resorted to a tried-and-true remedy. "Coffee." Jody walked through the hidden door and entered the warm and glowing storefront.

Stepping into the world of the living, Jody was met by a beautiful sight. Seated directly in front of him, sipping a latte was the shockingly beautiful form of a woman, red hair glistening in the shafts of sunlight, and her fit figure revealed in shadowy detail by the morning sun as it filtered through the gossamer fabric of her white dress. Mindlessly, he let the door slam behind him.

"Karen."

The young woman smiled with supple, ruby lips, and replied with inquisitive and puzzling eyes. "Hello?"

She was surprised to see him materialize out of seeming

nothingness. She paused and tilted her head to one side, studying him like she wasn't quite sure he was real.

Jody sheepishly shuffled over to her. "Are you here to meet your friend again?"

"Friend?" The puzzle pieces were slowly coming together for her. "Oh, yes, you're..."

"I'm sorry." His nervous interjection failed to exude the welcoming confidence he desperately wanted to portray. "I don't mean to be so nosey."

"Thank you." She held up her warm cup and shook it gently. Wide eyes and a giant smile proceeded an awkward giggle. "For the best coffee in the world."

"I may make it, but I don't believe that for a second. Someone as beautiful as yourself can find entertainment in a hundred other places than a dusty old coffee shop. So, why do you keep showing up here?"

"Don't be so presumptive," she scolded, "maybe I'm thirsty, and this is really good coffee." Jody nodded quietly in reply. "Fine, you're right." She gave up her pretense and her posture loosened into a more relaxed and open frame. "There's something about this place. I can't stay away."

"What do you mean?"

Her eyes darted around the room wildly. "This place, every detail, my friend told me about it. I didn't believe him at first, but when I came and saw... felt everything in here... I just can't stop thinking about it. Every book, every person, even you... I see in my dreams."

Jody was made uneasy by her urgent searching. "Who?"

"My friend? A younger guy, about your height..."

Karen's eyes were so deep, her voice so enthralling. He hung on every word she was saying, but he couldn't wait to hear about her dreams. "No, who... or what... else do you dream about... when you dream about this place?

Karen stopped and looked him squarely eye to eye. "... a boy. There was this little boy, in nickers and an ivy cap."

Jody's heart raced. He coughed to control his reaction. "A boy? I haven't seen any kids around today."

Karen grimaced, her eyes thinned and a foggy vail of distance fell over her stare. "Lying isn't becoming on you, Jody." Her face snapped quickly to her shoulder and a few stray tendrils of hair flowed in a nearly imperceptible draft. "Did you feel that?"

Jody shook his head no, but he did feel it. His entire right arm had cold goosebumps growing on it.

"Look, um, Jody. I can't do this now." In a flash she was stomping away clumsily on her one-inch heels, her figure still beautiful against the sun. Behind her, the Stabat Mater crescendoed and Jody shivered.

As the door clanged shut behind Karen, a porcelain mug slipped from its perch amongst the stacks of clean dishes on the top shelf behind the counter. Meg watched it fly from the shelf and dropped the drink she was making. It shattered on the floor, leaving broken shards and coffee mingled on the boards at her feet. Meg screamed. Her hands and arms quaked. It was thrown. There was no one there. Nothing touched it, but it was thrown.

CHAPTER
TEN

"It's okay, breathe." Jody placed reassuring hands on Meg's shoulders as she breathed violently into a crumpled paper bag. "Just breathe."

The concerned crowd had dispersed to their own seats. Jody had taken her to an empty table in the corner and there they sat, side by side. "I... can't... I... can't..."

"Yes, you can Meg, just breathe. Deep breaths... deep... slow... in...out...". He guided her back from her panic.

She lowered the bag from her face and looked over Jody's shoulder with quivering eyes. "I'm sorry, Jody..."

"Don't worry about the mug Meg."

"I'm sorry about the screaming. I just... I... I..."

"What? You just what?"

"I made a drink and I felt a tug at my pants so I looked down and..." A squeak of terror came up through her throat. "... there was this little boy."

Jody sat back in his chair in disbelief. He remembered Karen, she had gone without giving him any answers. But, he knew now that he wasn't crazy.

"Dude, is everything okay?" Billy rushed over in a flash to help in any way he could. He made an attempt at discretion, but his nerves turned his whisper into something more like a soft scream.

Jody looked up at him rather annoyed. "Yes, we're fine, and could you keep it down."

"Sure, um sorry." Billy shuffled softly around the table and noisily settled into an open chair. "So, is she having a panic attack or a bad grade or somethin'?"

"It's nothing, Billy." Meg snapped. "Just go, leave me alone."

"Oh, I see, so things are all normal then." He got up quickly. "I know it's my day off, but I'll just go hop in for her so things don't get backed up. You just sit here and make sure that... stays cool." He waved his index finger in Meg's general direction.

Jody nodded his approval.

"Jerk," Meg barked as he walked away.

"Hey now. You know he's not just a jerk. He's *my* jerk."

Meg returned his remark with a sideways glance and a half-hearted smile. "I know you guys have history, but your friend is a jerk, Jody Howard."

"That's fair." He smiled and nodded.

Meg took a sip of the ice water in front of her. "You weren't surprised."

"You nearly scared me to death. I almost fell out of my chair."

"No. You weren't surprised by what I saw. What's going on here, Jody?"

Jody shifted nervously in his seat. "Well..." He stalled for as long as he could, but it was apparent he couldn't run away from addressing the truth. "I didn't want to believe it. I'd never even considered the possibility before..."

A familiar cough interrupted his confession. He looked up and Billy called his attention to a gentleman standing by the coffee counter. "He wants to speak to you, personally. He says it's important."

Jody eyes transfixed on the curious individual. He cocked

his head to the side. There was something strangely familiar about this man, his bearded face, and his bald head was freshly shaven. His skin was light, not pasty but pallid in a way that asked for a few more hours of sun. He was dressed well, pressed blue jeans and a simple t-shirt covered by a navy-blue suit coat. His eyes seemed kind, and his demeanor decried a welcoming confidence. Dark and sharp pupils danced inside blue orbs, full of focus and determined purpose. All the pieces slowly came together in Jody's mind. He was finally able to place the man. This was the same gentleman that had handed Mr. Tipton a stack of cash just a few days prior and walked away with a rare copy of a book from the 1700's.

"Listen," Meg slammed her apron on the counter. "I'm out of here. This... whatever it is... is not normal." She intentionally looked Jody eye-to-eye. "I need normal."

Jody was speechless. There was nothing he could do but watch her storm out and have Billy pick up the pieces she left behind.

The bald man scanned the top shelves of each bookcase with particular care and intensity. Jody approached the man quietly, not wanting to spook him by somehow disturbing his concentration.

"May I help you with something?"

"Oh, yes. Allow me to introduce myself." He stretched out a calloused hand. "I'm Don Longworth, at least that's what your predecessor insisted on calling me."

Jody felt at ease looking into the man's face, and his voice was like warm velvet. "Nice to meet you, sir. What should I call you?"

"You may call me Don. I prefer familiarity over formality. I never quite understood Allen's insistence on distance. Truth is, I don't think he liked me very much."

Jody introduced himself and explained the curious circumstances surrounding how he came into possession of the coffee shop.

"Yes, I remember you. I was a good customer of Allen's... among other things. I hope our business is just as fruitful with you at the helm." His eyes scanned the bookshelves again while he spoke, as if hunting some hidden prey.

"I'm not sure how I've managed to miss the pleasure of meeting you before, Don." The bearded man's peculiar manner still had Jody mesmerized. His eyes followed the man's gaze as it danced around the room. He looked intently for those distinctive golden flecks he was sure he saw in them before, but today they were absent.

"The purchases I made from Allen were," he paused as he looked back at Jody, "of a less traditional nature, not your normal retail transaction. I am a collector, a serious collector. I love books, have always loved books. Words are amazing, powerful, and vibrant things. The words of great minds and hearts preserved on the page are as inspirational to me as any stone sculpture or oil painting in the halls of a museum. They speak to the heart, long after their author is dust and memory."

Jody remembered the name. It came up over and over again on the business ledger, always followed by large dollar transactions. Several seemed to come through at just the right time, just before the shop would dip into the red, that name, Donald Longworth, would appear on the page with a windfall.

"Normally, I would call him at his home, and we would arrange to meet here after hours, but this time I thought it best to stop by when I could meet you, face to face."

"I'd be more than happy to help you, sir. If there's anything you'd like me to look for and purchase for you..."

"Today, I'm here looking for something that Allen was supposed to have already purchased for me. It was an early copy of Dracula."

"Dracula, of course, I know exactly where it's at. I'd be

happy to get it for you." Jody sprang into action. He grabbed the ladder, methodically ascended the rickety rungs, and took the book ever so carefully from its place of honor high on the shelf.

The peculiar man's face was swept with relief. "Oh, it's here. You found it." Donald looked around the room at the employees and customers as they busied themselves with their routines. "Is there anywhere we could go...to be a bit more private?" His strong voice trailed off in embarrassment. "I'm afraid I'm not used to doing business quite so publicly."

"Sure, my office," Jody offered. "Right this way." The two walked into the old back room.

"Let us get down to brass tacks, Jody." The bearded man pulled out a pair of spectacles from his pocket and put then squarely on his nose as he received the book from Jody's hand. "How much do you want for it?"

Jody knew exactly how much Mr. Tipton had put into it. He bought it from the estate of a woman in New England for $8,000, a fraction of its value. It represented a good opportunity for profit, and could even fund the store's operations for months. But he knew this man knew Mr. Tipton, and he knew that if he could retain him as a client, he could come back and buy even more items, on a regular basis, just like he had for the old man. "I'll take $10,000 for it. I think that would be a fair price considering you had such a good relationship with Mr. Tipton."

"Ten thousand?" Mr. Longworth's voice boomed. "What a ridiculous sum." His head bobbed as he chuckled. "This book is worth fifteen if it's worth a penny, quite the nice piece." His aged fingers leafed through the delicate pages, skin touching paper like two old friends embracing one another. "I've always liked this shop, Jody. There's something peculiar about it, close to my heart. I must tell you; I like you too. You seem to have a solid head on your shoulders and a knack for business, just like your predecessor. I want to continue to do business with you, just like I did with Allen. If you provide me fair deals, I will pay you a fair price. Never-the-less, in honor of his memory, I will give you an extra fair price, just this once."

Jody's face betrayed the confusion in his mind. "I'm sorry, sir, what price?"

The bearded man took a worn blue checkbook from his back pocket and scribbled out a check quickly using a pen he grabbed from the bundle sitting on the desk. He carefully freed the slip of paper from its perforated binding and handed it to Jody.

The young man squinted as he read the script aloud. "Twenty thousand dollars," Jody stammered, dumbfounded.

"Not a penny less. I owe that much to Allen, to this place. I just can't bear to think it sinking into ruin." The bearded man embraced Jody's shoulder in his right hand with a surprisingly strong grip. "I hope we can do this many more times, Jody."

"I'd love to, sir. Anytime," Jody's fingers held it up in the light to get a better look.

"Good. I will hold you to that. But, for now, I have to go. I have an appointment across town in thirty minutes."

"Thank you, sir. Thank you." Jody winced under the vice-like grip of Mr. Longworth's hand. As the odd man left, Jody finally caught it, that same golden glint he had searched for earlier. It came out with the joy in the old man's voice.

A strange, unfamiliar feeling gripped Jody deep inside his bones. It was joy, unexpected, overflowing. He had never held such a sum of money in his hands at one time. Long after Don left, Jody sat there, still in his seat, dumbfounded. The old clock tolled the quarter hour, and Jody held the check up to the yellowing lamplight and read the words carefully again. "Twenty thousand dollars, signed Donald Longworth Tipton."

CHAPTER
ELEVEN

J ody wiped the dust off of the old grandfather clock with a white rag lightly sprayed with pledge. The polish soaked into the grain and slowly resuscitated the wood under the warm glow of the Study Hall's lights.

"I'm sorry that I left so abruptly yesterday. I just... I..." Meg had hoped waiting until closing time to meet with Jody would make it easier to deliver her mea culpa. She was mistaken.

Jody had spoken not a word as he went about his evening chores around the shop. The last client had long ago gone back to their place in the outside world, and the sign in the window dutifully turned to "closed."

"I feel like I'm drowning." Jody carefully folded his rag and placed it in a cupboard with the other cleaning supplies. "This place used to feel like home. Now I'm not sure I even recognize it anymore. It gives me the creeps and, now, it seems to be effecting my employees. I'm just trying to keep my head above water, and I'm looking for someone, anyone, I can trust."

Meg's fingers twirled tight curls into her dark disheveled locks as she watched Jody pace back and forth along the bookcases. "I know things are confusing, even scary right now, but I know I can help you with that." Her voice echoed across the large room. "You aren't the only one who feels an uneasy presence in this place. I've felt it. Billy feels it.. He was even wanting to bring in some kind of supernatural investigation group."

Jody drew closer, looked into her eyes, and smiled. "An investigation group?" He chuckled.

Meg's face turned stony and harsh. "I'm serious."

"No, no, no." Jody protested, begging the warmth to return to her eyes. "I'm laughing not because it's a dumb idea... I'm laughing because last week I would have felt it was a bad idea... and now... not so much."

Meg's harsh thin lips untangled into a pleasant line. "You are not alone."

Her words were assuring, but he still wasn't quite sure whether to trust her instincts or cling to the more familiar confines of logic. "You have kind eyes, Meg. They make me want to believe you."

"You don't have to believe my eyes. Believe your own. With things like this, the angst, the stress, it mostly comes from within yourself, from an unwillingness to trust in your own perception." Meg's skin tingled, the hair on her arms raised as he drew even nearer. Nervously, she turned her face toward the coffee bar and leaned away. "I'm sorry I'm..." she got up quickly and walked toward the register, her back towards him so as not to display the embarrassment written across her face. "I'm feeling a little dizzy. I must be a little dehydrated."

She pulled out a compact and looked in the tiny mirror for any embarrassing smudges or mistakes in her makeup. Her breath hitched as Jody touched her elbow with a warm, inviting hand, handing her a cold glass of ice water.

"I've been feeling pretty alone... through this... through... everything." He leaned back against the counter, gripping the bullnose edge tightly in sweaty, unseen fingers. "You know, speaking of alone...I was thinking about going..."

Meg finished her water, eyes closed, and interrupted Jody's

sentence with the sound of glass landing heavy on the counter-top. "You know sometimes," she groaned. "It would be nice if you could let me go through one night shift without asking me out." Jody couldn't even apologize before she was barking at him from the door. "Just friends, Jody. I've told you... so many times before. That's all I can take right now. I just want... normal things, Jody."

He stood there long after the door had slammed, still gripping the cold countertop, shoulders slumped, heart beating loudly in his ears.

"I'm a blistering, white hot mess." He hid his face hard in his hands and let a muffled scream out into the empty room.

As his voice stopped echoing from pillar to post, a sharp rattling noise tore through the room causing Jody to nearly jump out of his skin. Rap, rap, rap! The sound cracked again, shaking the front door. Jody ran and peeked through the window pane to see what lay beyond the threshold. A pretty porcelain smile crowned by red hair peeked back at him.

"Hey! Can you let me in?" her muffled voice filtered through the glass.

They sat in silence for the longest time, sipping steaming hot mugs of coffee until Jody could take it no more. "So...what are you doing tonight... here?"

"A midnight stroll... I live not too far from here, just a few blocks down, on the 6th floor. It's a tiny place, not like where I come from. I get a little stir crazy sometimes, a walk helps me find my center."

"Center..." Jody sipped his coffee his eyes still transfixed on the beautiful young lady, watching her every move intently, seeking some gentle tell, an unspoken sign to give insight into the meaning behind her odd behavior. "You... keep strange hours Karen. I give you that."

"Trust me, I wish I didn't. I'd give anything to just get a full night's sleep."

"Insomnia?"

"Yes," The coffee cup caressed her ruby lips again, accepting yet another gossamer arc of color as payment for its patience in her hands. "Something like that." Jody's eyes still never moved, barely blinked. She shifted uneasily in her seat. "Fine, let me be honest with you, Jody."

"I wish you would."

"I can't sleep. I can't rest. I can barely concentrate most of the time, all because I'm drawn here."

"Here?"

"This coffee shop, this chair, right here, all the time. I go to work, and I think about it. I lay down in bed and I can't get it off my mind. I want, I need, to be right here."

"Why?"

"I have no idea. It's been like this for days, maybe weeks. I don't know. I just know that when I'm not here. I want to be here. I toss, I turn, I get out of bed and I walk down the side-walk, here, almost every night. Tonight, I saw your lights were still on so I tried knocking, and tonight, you opened the door. So, I, get to be here."

"Do you feel better?"

"No." The matter-of-fact nature of her statement made them both chuckle. "I don't know why. I thought I would feel better, but...nothing."

"I don't think this coffee is going to help your nerves."

"I need a drink." She was shockingly insistent. Jody reached for her mug. "No, something stronger than coffee, much stronger."

Jody was about to bid her goodnight when she reached out and grabbed his hand. Her fingers were warm from the mug, and her firm touch immediately captured his interest. "Why don't you come with me?"

"I'm sorry, Karen, but I don't drink... a promise I made a

long time ago to an old friend." They were the last words Jody wanted to say.

They were so full of angst and pent-up stress that Karen refused to hear them. "Nonsense, just come with me. You're already closed. There's more to life than books and coffee."

"I thought you wanted to be here, right here."

The statement gave Karen pause. "I thought I did, but I still feel... off, not the relief I was hoping for. Please, come on, you don't even have to drink. The D.D. gets free Coke."

CHAPTER
TWELVE

Billy walked the sidewalk along the dark urban canyon on a mission. His ambling gate made him seem more full of alcohol than purpose. His eyes darted this way and that, around corners, down alleyways, constantly mumbling to himself. "Come on, come on, come on." Seemingly almost by accident, he came to the doorway of The Study Hall and pulled at the door. It was locked.

"Come on, man!" He tugged once again but the old door stubbornly refused to give way. He pressed his nose against the giant bay windows and cupped his hands around his face to keep the surrounding light pollution from distorting his view. There were a few dim lights on in the back, but no motion, no discernible sign of life at all. "Dude! Come on. You've got to be here somewhere. You only closed," he desperately looked at his watch. "Two...yeah, two hours ago." Spinning nervously on his heels he marked out a tiny circle in the pavement shoving his right hand into his pocket and searching. He grasped it at last, pulled the key from his pants, and shoved it into the lock.

A quick flick of the switch flooded the front room with light as the door slammed behind him. "Hello! Are you in here?" He rushed back to the storage room, but there was no one. "Ah, come on!"

Thumbs tapped hurriedly on his cell phone screen, beating out a line of text underneath a received message that read, "Heading out." The phone dinged and a new message appeared. "I'm fine, see you tomorrow."

"Come on!" he exclaimed, dropping his arms to his side in defeat.

The legs of an old wooden chair screamed into the empty room as Billy took a seat and lay his forehead flat against the table, chest still heaving from his rushed efforts. "This... is... exactly... why... we...can't... have... nice... things." His fist wrapped rhythmically against the table as he spoke, bouncing his head up and down.

He propped himself up wearily on his elbows and tapped out another message. "You told me you wouldn't do that again the last time."

Soon, the phone chimed again. "I AM FINE! No stupid decisions."

"Fine, I'm not chasing you all over the city," Billy grumbled.

He wandered into the back of the store to start turning out the lights. It was colder, darker somehow than he felt it had been earlier. It felt empty, which made him feel empty. "I hate being alone in this place, man."

His fingers wandered from surface to surface, seeking some mischief to distract him from the gnawing concern for his friend, and the intrusive thoughts of the cooling, contorted body of Mr. Tipton lying alone for who knows how long in the back room. A thousand horrible thoughts and a hundred nasty dark feelings churned in him and around him.

The place felt stale, but charged, like he was walking through a dank electric fog. There was no peace here, there never was, but it was especially pronounced when there were no other people there to distract from the emptiness. He walked over to the record player, turned it on, and carefully placed the needle in proper position. The exquisitely beautiful and lonely tones of the Stabat Mater began to fill the room. He walked back out into the storefront, grabbed himself a candy bar from behind the counter and sat himself down to eat. Food was his coping mechanism, the salve that distracted him from the woes of life, food and beer, of course.

Billy ate, enjoying the sweet and salty flavors washing over his tongue. The snap and groan of peanuts rumbled through his head with every bite, and he enjoyed just that, every single bite. He licked a dry and cracking finger and breathed in deeply, expecting the aroma of freshly roasted peanuts, but in its place, was something quite different. The fragrance invoked a strong feeling that engulfed his entire body, like a warm hug. His lungs were filled with the sweetness of an amazingly distinctive feminine floral scent. "Who would that be?"

He turned, expecting to see someone, anyone. Instead, there was no one. Billy coughed. His throat began to burn and tingle under the intensity of the floral fumes.

"Huh? What?" He couldn't control his coughing, face turning red, gasping for air. "What...is...this?" The sweet smell, like lavender oil, became so sweet in his nostrils it turned his stomach.

As suddenly as the smell came, it left, dissipating into nothingness. Billy froze. Out of the corner of his eye, a figure moved then stopped and casually stood facing the bookcase along the wall. Stiff as a statue, he stayed perfectly still. He dared not turn to look. A chill ran down his spine.

"She shouldn't be there."

She was an older woman, with bark like skin, hard and wrinkled. She wore a light-colored dress that spilled over her hips all the way down past her ankles. The figure turned and walked down one of the bookcase isles. Billy finally gave in to the raging temptations of curiosity, and looked directly and intently upon her.

The woman's hair was highlighted by streaks of grey. The sleeves of her dress were long and trimmed with lace. The dress was wispy, almost translucent. She moved toward the back of the shop and turned the corner around the bookcase.

Billy gave chase. He walked quickly down the aisle. The smell of lavender trailing behind her was so strong it caused him to cough again. He turned the corner after her, and he stopped. She was gone. He walked swiftly back to the front of the store and carefully scanned every aisle. He looked down the empty street through one of the bay windows. She was nowhere to be found.

"Where did you go?"

Billy's hands began to shake. His heart pounded in his chest. Anxiety coursed through his veins like fire.

"Don't do this, don't do this, don't do this..." His mantra stopped abruptly. He was interrupted by the warm squeeze of a cold, dead hand around his own.

"Don't look."

A growling, muffled female voice whispered in his ear. It was so shocking, so out of place. A wisp of cold air flitted around his head. He could sense the old hag's presence as standing hairs followed her movement across his skin. Her breath stank of lavender and blew cold against his mouth, so very cold, so very dank. He felt her soft lips gently brush against his.

"No!" he flailed at the emptiness that surrounded him. "Stay away from me! You can't come in here. You can't have me. Do you hear me!?"

Billy shook, his whole body trembled. Instinctively, he turned to look behind him. There, standing at the other side of the table, was the wispy old woman. Her vague, stern stare pierced his soul. He screamed and the phantom disappeared into the back room.

Words escaped him. All of the nerve endings in his body seemed to be firing at once. Finally, words erupted from his mouth. "What the...?"

Slowly, on wobbly knees, he began to back out of the room, heading toward the front door.

"That face, I've seen that face before. I know I have." He rattled on to himself, no longer in doubt of everything he had suspected about this place for so long. Eyes firmly fixed on the back room, he never looked behind him or diverted his gaze, even when opening the door and locking it back.

THIRTEEN

Quiet and dark, the walls held Meg, close, safe, secure, with only the flitting light from the occasional passing car offering the specter of motion as they slid politely from one wall to another. Meg lay still, cocooned by cool, colorful sheets in floral patterns.

Her iPhone lay in its appointed and orderly position 3 inches from the edge of her night stand, face up. It flashed, vibrated and squawked the notification of a new text message. She lay there, silently staring at the ceiling for three more tones, refusing to yield her repose to the outside world. On the fourth, she relented and grabbed the offending instrument with groggy contempt.

The screen showed a puke emoji, with the text "You have 1 new message from D-Bag." She rolled her eyes and the phone vibrated again. "You have 2 new messages from D-Bag."

"Ugh, wait a second!"

She opened the thread and the two messages rolled up into her line of sight. "Help!" and "Call me!"

"Hello," she moaned. "No, Billy, what?" Her tone was sharp and short. "No, I just fell asleep." She pounded the bed silently with her fist. "Listen, if something's really wrong just call your man-crush, Jody!"

She reached over and tapped her touch lamp. "What do you mean he won't answer? He always answers." Meg sat up in her bed, tugging at the pillows bunching against the headboard behind her. "An old woman?" Meg was sleepy, but she knew she wasn't that sleepy. "She did what? No way!" Her disbelief was met with such a heart wrenching, impassioned rebuke that her eyes widened, and her eyebrows crossed. "Okay, chill, chill."

Meg looked around the room as she stalled for time with awkward hums. Her eyes fell on the closet door as Billy shared his idea. "You really think that's smart? Tonight?" She stood up. "Just wait a second...Yes, I know I can find it. Hold on...If you really think it will help us get to the bottom of this. Yes, yes, just hold on, I will find it."

Meg could tell by the tone in Billy's voice that he didn't quite believe her. "Give me thirty minutes. I'll see you soon. Bye."

The phone clicked and Meg walked over to her closet. With a wince and no small amount of consternation, she flew the door open. Nothing fell out. That was a pleasant surprise. She stretched hard up on her tip toes but couldn't reach the very top shelf. It was just too tall.

"Fine," she grumbled aloud.

Her delicate frame drug a chair from her desk over to the closet doorway. Carefully, she climbed up and balanced herself on the teetering makeshift step stool. Her hands fumbled and moved objects about until, at last, she stopped. The thin box rattled with a familiar clunky din. A smile of victory grew across her face as she climbed down, clutching the slender white box.

Meg got dressed and started out the door but stopped in her tracks.

"Almost forgot...".

She stepped back in her room and grabbed the thin white box she had left on her bed. She sighed, "Why am I even doing this for that... ugh!"

CHAPTER
FOURTEEN

"I got here as soon as I could." Meg saw a whitewashed face sitting before her. "You look like you've seen a..."

"Really?" Billy was not amused. He was sitting in the middle of the sidewalk, legs crossed, watching the locked storefront door with near religious devotion.

"Well, it's true, isn't it?"

"As God is my witness Meg, it is so true. So very, very true!" A smile broke across his pale face and he leapt to his feet. With every word he became happier and more excited. "My dudette! We have a confirmed full-bodied apparition inside our very own place of business."

"And this excites you?"

"Yes! I mean, no, it terrifies me... scared me snotless in there, but now," He could barely contain himself and grabbed her by the shoulders and danced an awkward waltz around her. "Now, we have the opportunity of a lifetime." He could tell by her blank stare that he wasn't quite making sense to her. "To make contact with a willing, and ready, honest to goodness ghost with a capital G!"

"Well..." Meg stared down Billy until the smile drooped from his face.

"Well... what?"

She slapped at his arm with her free hand. Anger, tears, hatefulness, were all familiar smoke screens she had mastered from her youth. "Well, get us in there and off of this ridiculous sidewalk."

"Ouch!, okay, calm down." Bill fumbled with the lock and stepped through the threshold, back into the lair of whatever that thing is. He had spent years developing a smoke screen to hide his fears and insecurities too. It was bad humor.

"You know, you're lucky I'm here with you tonight. I can protect you. I'm a supernatural force of nature," Billy laughed. "Eh?! Am I right?"

Meg rolled her eyes. "You pronounced 'idiot' wrong."

"But for reals, I'm part of this whole parapsychological organization, club thing."

"Don't you have to be able to spell 'parapsychological' to be in the club?"

"I can't, but they let me in anyway." He helped Meg set aside the white box as she laid out the wooden board, carefully centered on the table. "Its more of an organization really, not a club so much."

"So what do you do exactly?"

"I'm a hunter. We hunt ghosts. I'm kind of a natural sensitive."

Meg studied his expression carefully. He wasn't joking. "You're a...ghost hunter?"

"Yeah, pretty much, mmm hmm. I can sense things that others can't, energies and spirits, emotions."

Meg could not believe her ears. "What a strange, strange man."

Billy had proven himself many things in the past. He was incompetent, unpunctual, even inappropriate. There were many things that Billy could have revealed about himself at any given moment in time and she would not have even so much as batted an eyelash, but Billy the supernaturally gifted sensitive was not one of them. She was flabbergasted. "Did the ghost do anything to you?"

"Yes," he searched for a delicate way to put what happened, but there was none. "She tried to kiss me, I think."

"An undead old hag lady tried to kiss you?"

"Yes."

"You are such... a pervert. That is so wrong. How can I..."

Billy clapped his hands together and began dancing to the beat of his own drum just inches from Meg. "Hey baby!" His eyes squinted and voice crunched in a comical interpretation. "I'm just a love machine..."

Meg shoved him aside. "Ew, get off me, you're so....disgusting. Get off"

"Okay, okay, sorry, I'll knock it off." Billy shook himself dramatically and tried to center his raging emotions. Without warning or fanfare, he pulled out a chair and commanded Meg to sit. She was shocked and complied like a child scolded in the schoolyard.

"The plan for tonight..." Billy placed the simple wooden triangle in the center of the board. "...is to ask questions and get answers." He ran a finger over the large black title ornately emblazened across the top of the board. "This, is the answer box." The announcement and flamboyant presentation drew Meg's undivided attention. "Our hotline to the netherworld."

She giggled. "Sorry." She hid her mouth politely with modest embarrassment, "We're going to use a Ouija board?" Even though she dutifully brought the game herself, she still couldn't believe how ridiculous it sounded.

"Yeah, don't you remember playing this as a kid?" Billy's reply bordered on incredulous. "Haven't you ever done this? It works."

"So you're serious." Meg drummed nervously with her thumb on the table. "We're really going to do this?"

"Yes," Billy remained stoic as the grave. "Give me your hands."

The mournful strains of the Stabat Mater began wafting through the air. At first it was soft, then louder, and louder still. Billy could scarcely believe his ears. He wanted to run. He wanted to scream. That beautiful and creepy song somehow touched every weird thing that had happened to him.

Meg was near tears. Old fears, freshly buried, clawed back into her chest, chilling her blood. She wanted to put up a strong front, but deep inside the battle to hold it all in was a lost cause. She stammered breathlessly. "Oh my, oh my, oh my,"

The door to the back office flew open with a loud boom. They gasped.

"Ok, calm down." Billy squeezed Meg's hands tightly in his own. "We don't need extra negative energy. We don't know what we're dealing with here exactly."

Meg scooted as close to the table as she could and struggled to calm herself.

"Alright then, I want you to close your eyes," Billy continued. "Clear your mind of everything, all of your concerns, all of your fears, everything that's happened tonight. Let it all drift away from your consciousness. When you've cleared your mind, open your eyes."

Meg squinted hard, struggling to calm the torrent of fear inside her. Slowly, she opened her eyes, first one and then the other.

"Carefully, place your fingers on the planchette with mine."

The heart shaped wooden planchette sat solemnly on the board. It was perfectly centered within the arc of the letters printed across the top. Hands layered one by one on top of the strange wooden implement. It became the focus, the center of all of their mental energy. They were reaching out, wanting to know more, needing answers.

Billy laid out a roadmap for what they were about to experience. "I'm going to ask questions of any spirits that might be around us," If they are here, they will move the planchette to the word, number, or letters to give us their answer. I know it might be tempting, but please, do not try to force it to move by yourself. Let it move on its own. Just keep an open and clear mind, and no matter what happens, do not let go of the planchette."

Billy took a deep breath. "We come in search of the spiritual realm. We want to communicate with you. We have questions and are seeking answers. Are there any spirits here who wish to communicate with us?"

The sound of their own raspy breathing patted gently from wall to wall. It filled the air around the small wooden board. It was like a storm, a giant storm brewing around the center of the universe, and that center of the universe was heavy under the touch of their fingertips. The planchette shifted. It scooted across the board with a heavy scraping sound that pierced the wall of breath. At first it moved sporadically in spits and starts, then one long smooth plodding motion. It settled on one of the few complete words on the board. "Yes."

"Are you the old woman that scarred me earlier tonight?"

The planchette moved again. This time it drug itself to the opposite side of the board. "No."

"Who are you?" Meg asked impatiently.

The planchette moved slowly across the black lettering. The young supplicants mouthed each letter as it was identified by the mystical device. It methodically pointed out the letters "f-i-l-i-o." Then it stopped.

"Filio?" Meg wondered aloud. "What's that mean?"

Billy squeezed his eyes tightly before opening them again. He had hoped it would somehow magically transport him away from his uncomfortable situation. "I think it might be Latin," he groaned.

"Latin?" Meg questioned. "Are you sure it's..."

Before she could finish her sentence, Billy cut her off, asking another question of the invisible ethereal presence. "What do you want?"

The planchette took off again, this time faster and more erratic. Once again, the two friends mouthed the letters and tried to make sense of them. "Fac me vere tecum flere." It stopped.

"More Latin?" Meg asked.

Billy shrugged his shoulders. "I really have no idea. Maybe... um...What is your name?" They both watched intently as their fingers moved along with the planchette, guided by some unseen force. It spelled out a name. "T-I-P-T-O-N"

Meg and Billy looked wide-eyed at one another. "Mr. Tipton?" they exclaimed in unison.

Meg's voice boomed. "We don't understand what you're trying to tell us. Could you tell us again? Help us understand."

The planchette made even quicker work of its trek across the board. "Fac me vere tecum flere." Then three complete circles clockwise around the board and it stopped hard on the word "Yes."

Meg gasped. Her expression froze in a grotesque and silent scream. Billy instinctively tracked her line of sight. Standing between Meg and Billy was a small boy dressed in a dark overcoat. His arm was extended, and his hand rested on top of Meg's over the planchette. He mouthed something to them, but no one could hear him. Billy could hear his own heart beating in his chest, pounding a rhythmic cadence of fear in his ear drums. The ghostly child tried again to communicate, this time screaming his words clearly for everyone at the table. The voice was that of a young boy, but it coursed through the room like an overdriven stereo system. "Fac me vere tecum flere!"

They could see he was crying. As he wept, tears streamed from his eyes and flowed down his reddening face, but they again could hear nothing. Then, as suddenly as he came, he disappeared.

Meg screamed. She pulled her hand from the planchette and used it to cover her gaping mouth.

"That was..." Meg began.

"Full bodied apparition number two, wow!" Billy stammered. "I wish I would have known it was coming like that."

"As opposed to what," Meg replied indignantly, "the disappearing creepy shopping lady that reeks of lavender?"

"Okay, we've got a serious problem here." Billy had to distance himself from the situation. He couldn't even begin to comprehend and absorb the crazy things he just saw, felt, and heard with his own senses. He stood up quickly from the table. "We have ghosts, like real ghosts, like more than one."

"Do you know what he wants?" Meg asked. "What was it saying?"

"I have no idea, no more than you."

Billy leapt from the table and darted toward the back room. "I know where we can look for some answers." He disappeared into the darkened doorway and emerged moments later with the record sleeve. "Here it is," he proclaimed. "This is the closest thing I have to a Latin-English dictionary, believe it or not." He laid it out on top of the Ouija board.

CHAPTER
FIFTEEN

Jody drifted into consciousness from a deep dark abyss, pinned to the earth by some unseen force. His left arm would not respond, dead to his command, although it radiated a piercing hot pain all the way up through his shoulder. He tried his right. It could still move. He reached out, fumbling to identify the strange force that held him captive. "Ouch!" A shard of glass bit into his thumb and sliced free a flap of skin. He continued groping in the relative darkness for the object that pinned him hard to the earth.

At last, he sat a trembling, bleeding hand onto a cold object, a steel rod, twisted and mangled. He struggled against it and grunted loudly, heaving all his might against the rod, but it held him fast.

Blood rushed back into his head, behind a piercing headache, he regained his sight. With renewed vision, he identified the object. It was the mangled remains of a truck door. He was upside down in the cab of their old red truck. The roof was gone, only leaves and grass lay beneath him, wet with blood and fluids leaking from the engine. He was trapped, with only enough mobility to writhe in pain. Mingled with his moans, the downcast melodies of the Stabat Mater surrounded him in the crushed truck.

"Dad! Dad I'm..." No other words would come out. He tried to scream but his paralyzed vocal cords would not comply. His father was still seated beside him, upside down, trapped by the seatbelt, gripping tight a bent steering wheel now jammed up into his chest, blood slowly but steadily dripping from the gaping cavity where half of his head once was.

"Daddy!"

He could see the man's face. "Look at me! Right here, just look right here." Those sparkling, steely blue-grey eyes called to him. He could feel himself slipping back down into the darkness. He struggled against it, trying to focus, trying to not think about his dad's lifeless body. "Right here, stay right here, with me. I'm not going anywhere."

∼

J ody sat straight up in bed. A cold clammy sweat dripped from his pores, causing his flannel pajama bottoms to cling to his skin. He threw off the covers and swung his feet over the side of the mattress, gasping for breath.

"No, no, no...Daddy."

He rubbed his eyes with open palms. They were wet with tears. He felt ashamed somehow. He was crying. Deep inside his heart and mind he underwent a shocking metamorphosis from young teen into a grown man. This rapid internal maturity from childhood to adulthood recurred over and over again in his sleep. Every detail of the dreams faithfully portrayed that horrible evening in the most vivid minutia, save one small and recent change. Ever since Mr. Tipton had died, the Stabat Mater was there, always.

He looked up toward the ceiling and allowed his senses to drink up the familiarity of the now, the present and peaceful solitude of his bedroom. The fog of the past lifted and cleared from his tired eyes. The muscles in his arms tensed as a new, strange sensation filled his ears. Water dripped and fell rhythmically nearby, like a torrent of rain only feet away. The steady patter of the artificial rain falling on ceramic tile was accented by a delicate feminine voice humming a haunting tune only slightly off key.

He became fully present and aware. The now was different. He had experienced something he had never done before, and now the world was not the same. Every piece of furniture, every feature of the world around him was unchanged, but now, as he sat up in bed, the very atoms he touched seemed turned on edge. Something deep down to the core of his existence was different.

Searching for the answer, he mulled the events of the last few hours. Swimming through a fog of distorted images, he recounted and ordered them as best he could.

First, he took Karen to the movies at the Levee, the ten o'clock showing of some chick flick he normally would have never considered spending money on under normal circumstances. Second, a walk along the River Walk and across the purple bridge into downtown Cincinnati. His legs were sore, that was a long walk, a lot longer than he was accustomed to.

Then, third, a memory of a distinct discomfort in the seat of his pants, and an image of a spindly wooden bar stool. She had taken him by the hand into a little hole in the wall dive bar not far from the river. The stools at the bar were awful. He couldn't wait to get out of there.

Fourth, they left, and walked back across the bridge. They stopped halfway across and looked at the river twinkling under the city lights. He was exhausted, not feeling very well. Fifth, they... no that couldn't be right. No, it wasn't. Fifth, they laughed. He felt a little tipsy, but he felt something more... happy. He hadn't been happy in such a long time. It felt like a fresh breeze across his soul, like the smell of honeysuckle on a clean summer morning. All the self-doubt, all of the fear had been burnt away under the blazing light of that one laugh.

Sixth, he gave up. Maybe he had just given up on Meg because he was tired of the frustration. Her rejection was a rhythm in his universe as faithful as the rising of the sun. He longed for comfort and acceptance. Meg would not give it to him. She would only push him away. This time she pushed him, hard, right into... number Seven.

He kissed her. He pulled Karen close, and she pressed her soft and delicate lips into his own. She melted onto his chest and rested her head against him. She melted into his thoughts, his dream, then into his bed.

An involuntary belch brought up a noxious concoction through his windpipe and into his nostrils that wreaked of alcohol. The effervescent fumes clung to his skin. He could not wipe it away by hand and he could not remove the acrid taste from his mouth no matter how many times he raked his drying tongue against his front teeth.

"What have I done?" He mulled over the question in the quiet darkness, drinking in the smell of her perfume and free flowing meter of her shower song.

The cellphone, lain carelessly on the nightstand, began to vibrate and ring. Jody reached for it. The name "Meg" was emblazoned boldly across the screen in bright white text, but he never answered it.

He smelled of alcohol. His breath, his skin, everything, even his hands. The noxious odor gave him chills. It pulled at him, from somewhere deep in the pit of his stomach, grounding him, pulling him back into a past he'd rather forget, closer to that metal box hidden just beneath the edge of the bed where he sat.

"I want you." An airy growl crawled up his spine, imbedded in his mind. "I want you, Jody." Dark, dead, hidden inside his own brain. It chilled him, drove him. His hand reached down and cupped the bottom of the bed rail.

"No! Leave it!" Jody groaned and pulled his hand back, trapping it in place on his lap with a vice like grip from his opposite fingers around his own clammy wrist. He shook himself and waited, alone, in the dark bedroom, watching the light escaping around the frame of the door to the bathroom, listening to the distant sound of water.

The pitter patter of artificial rain had stopped. Before him, silhouetted against the soft white light of the adjoined bathroom, a beautiful redheaded goddess stood, looking down on his pitiful state of confusion and remorse. Her supple skin glistened with small rippling beads of shower water.

"I didn't mean to wake you," her sultry voice called to him from deep inside her slowly heaving chest. "But I'm so glad I did."

Karen grabbed his wrist and wrapped his arms around her wet, naked body. Meg was forgotten, the box was forgotten, and every time she called that night he ignored the buzzing.

CHAPTER
SIXTEEN

The morning star shone brightly over the bustling streets of Cincinnati. The Queen City begged to clear her head with a cup of hot morning brew. The Study Hall opened its doors and yawned wide to meet this need. Meg, too, yawned. She opened wide and begged for life and air to fill her chest, to spark her mind and give her power to exorcise the images carved into her mind's eye last night. Her hands fumbled, mixing coffees for clients as they hurried off to work.

Billy fared no better. "Six a.m. is way too close to four a.m." Billy never seemed to complain about late nights when he was partying. He had always worn morning grog like a badge of honor, a testament to the enduring power of youthful virility.

Meg offered him neither grace nor reprieve. Mercy did not come easy to Meg. It was a precious commodity she preferred to offer men of more humble repute, never considering those most flawed might be in need of a double portion. Her elbow hit the coffee she had just made and it careened across the counter. Billy reached over and grabbed the mug as it began its flight off of the countertop.

Jody snapped a dishrag in Bill's direction. "Good catch." He leaned in heavily against the countertop right beside Meg.

"What do you think I should tell this guy? He'll be here any minute."

Meg handed a hot coffee to a dapper middle-aged man dressed in a pin striped suit. "I don't know what the big deal is. Just tell him that the ghost of your former boss is stuck in a child-like state and can only talk to you in Latin." She was extra snarky this morning, and it showed in her sharp delivery.

"Come on Meg. I'm serious. This is no joke." Billy had convinced him to call in an expert to deal with their supernatural infestation. He was completely conflicted between the ridiculousness of a supernatural expert and the common-sense, matter-of-fact nature that such a person would be the best suited to deal with matters concerning an unwanted haunting. "He should be here any time now." Jody bit nervously at his lip.

"You called a U.C. professor, not 9-1-1. Give him some time," Billy croaked. It was all the comfort and support he could offer on such little rest absent inebriation.

"Jody?"

He immediately snapped to attention. A raven-haired woman on three-inch heels, wearing a pin-striped pant suit sauntered up to the counter. The sound of her tall heels pounding into the floorboards lent an aire of authority beyond what one might attribute to her slender frame and fair features.

"I'm Dana Austin."

His face contorted as perception slowly molded into reality behind his eyes. "You're... Professor Austin?"

"Yes."

Jody didn't know why he had assumed Professor Dana Austin would have been a man. There was no logical reason a woman couldn't hold a position of power, fighting monsters and demons, dredging the darkest corners of the cities and banishing wraiths and phantoms with overwhelming force. He felt unexpectedly ashamed, like he had somehow vindicated every college speaker barking behind their bully pulpit about the evils of an inherently male dominated society by this one simple misplaced assumption. He didn't want to embarrass himself so he said the first thing that came into his head.

"And you're a woman."

"Duh," Billy chuckled as he cashed out another customer.

The distinguished professor cleared her throat, choking down a smirk. "Yes, I am. I'm glad Billy was able to help us get in touch with one another."

"That's Billy, always ready to help and full of surprises." Jody wiped his hands dry and put away his apron.

"He's a valuable member of our team, does great work for us." She motioned in acknowledgement of the bustling crowded room. "Is there somewhere we can go to talk a little more privately?"

"Yes, step into my office." Jody led her into the dingy recesses of the back room and hastily offered her a squeaky chair, which was politely declined. Jody nervously sat in the chair himself and watched her as she stood, saying nothing. Her eyes were as big as saucers, her neck craned as if trying to spy some precious lost object in the corners of the room.

"We, um, that is my staff and I," he started awkwardly, "have been noticing some peculiar things going on around the shop."

"Peculiar?" The black-haired lady asked in a pencil thin tone, still engaged in a search that had stolen most of her attention. "Strange noises? Objects moving?"

"Noises," he replied quickly.

"What kind of noises?"

"Latin." He said flatly.

"Latin?" Ms. Austin's head snapped back to Jody. "I'm sorry, did you say Latin?"

"Yes, we've heard some disembodied voices, well *a* disembodied voice anyway, speaking Latin. That, and we've seen a couple of specters." Jody felt like an utter buffoon rattling off his description of the encounters. But he told the details faithfully, just as he had remembered them. "It's foolish I know," he concluded. "We're probably all just crazy."

"No, no Mr. Howard, you are neither foolish nor crazy." She turned her gaze slightly toward the ceiling resuming her radar like scan. "Contrary to what your mother or father may have told you, there *are* such things as ghosts."

Her eyes made him uncomfortable. They were cold and steely, her stare other worldly. "Who are they?" she asked.

"Who?"

"The boy and the woman, who are they?"

Jody swallowed hard. "I-I, um I don't know"

Ms. Austin breathed in heavily. "I think I believe you, Mr. Howard." Jody didn't realize that the efficacy of his testimony was in question, but he felt somehow relieved that she had deemed to give his word credence. "I think you have a very real...situation. In fact, I think you don't even know the half of it. Something is amiss here. Something is hiding. It is dark. It is powerful, and it is hiding."

"It hid just fine for years. It's not hiding anymore, it's showing off." Jody shifted to the front of his chair.

"Did it?" her eyes slowly scanned the baseboards. "What has awakened it?" She looked back again toward Jody. "Or, what has awakened you to it?"

Jody sat dumbfounded at both prospects. A new world was unfolding before him. He found himself looking about the room just like Ms. Austin. Everyday objects became hiding places for manifestations from the beyond. His mind perceived ghosts in every book, haunts in every drawer.

"I think we should conduct a formal investigation, the sooner the better."

"I don't know, Ms Austin." Jody balked at her presumptive tact. "I'm exhausted, my staff is exhausted. I think we need some time."

She lurched over and leveled her stony face to his. "I can't impress upon you enough the gravity of your situation. This energy," she waived her hands violently around her head, "is malevolent, a special kind of malevolence I don't often see." A perfectly manicured nail danced delicately across a chair back. The woman felt the air with her soul, eyes closed, paying only attention to the unseen. "There is another here." Her lips scrunched hard together. "He is dark. He is strange." She gasped and quickly stared Jody straight in the eyes. "It will take me a few days to coordinate my whole team. But I can't impress upon you enough, I'm getting a very strong psychic impression of this thing's intent... this dark spirit, Mr. Howard, wants you dead."

SEVENTEEN

"Death is not the end." Those words had never sounded as beautiful and meaningful as they did coming from Karen's lips. She crunched at a hard breadstick and gazed at him from smiling eyes. "You should go ahead and order something. You're starving, I can tell."

"I need to wait. He said he wanted to meet me for lunch." He fiddled with his collar. The coat and tie scene was not a place that he normally took his midday meal.

"Take a deep breath, be natural." She caressed his cold hand. "You're going to get to the bottom of this, and you've got time."

The stress of the whole situation was weighing on him. He wasn't sleeping well, tossing and turning, dealing with those horrible dreams, walking on eggshells at the Study Hall. He had no peace. He had no sanctuary.

"I am the end." The snake hissed into his soul. Jody pulled at his ear and massaged the tender cartilage of his earlobe, unwilling to scratch at the itching inside the canal like a psychopath, as he sat tucked behind a well appointed table in the most expensive restaurant he had ever had the pleasure of patronizing.

"It wants me dead." Jody's grip tightened around the thick linen napkin. It crumpled and creased in his hands, no longer the pristine pressed white field of cloth presented to him on his place setting.

"She said it was going to take a few days to get everything in place. Do what you have to do now."

Jody closed his eyes and opened them again. She was still there. A few weeks ago she wasn't even within his realm of consciousness and now this beautiful, supportive woman, was still there. She wasn't a dream. She was real. He wanted and needed more things in life that were real.

"Oh! Here he comes." She pushed her chair in and kissed his forehead. "I'll see you tonight."

Jody rose. A quick turn and firm handshake later, he was seated across from a mysterious man and his most generous benefactor, about to have an unimaginably awkward conversation about a subject no sane small business owner in need would ever breech. A young waitress in a pink blouse and black slacks sat a glass of deep red wine in front of Jody.

"Thank you." He nodded with an obligatory grunt. He pawed at his slice of hot sourdough bread and smeared on a pat of butter. "Things aren't right there, Don. It shouldn't be this hard."

Donald ate, eyes fixated on the table, first one piece of warm buttery sourdough, then another. He washed them down with a giant swig from his glass of sweet tea before he let his eyes rest on Jody's concerned face. "Starting a business is hard. I know it was up and running before, but you're really starting over fresh, just yourself at the helm."

"It's not the business." Jody's fingers played with the cool, sweaty glass before him. "It's something else."

Donald settled his napkin into his lap. "Something... different?"

His demeanor was calm, his countenance unflinching.

Calloused fingers scratched at his beard around a knowing upturned smile. His attention settled, unwavering, on Jody.

"It's nothing like I was expecting." Jody's voice cracked. "People are going to get hurt."

"What exactly is going on, Jody?"

His voice quivered. "I've stumbled on some of Allen's personal affects at the store..."

"Stumbled?"

"No not..." Jody huffed in frustration. He rubbed the ridge of his nose with one hand trying to alleviate the growing headache radiating around his skull.

"What affects?"

"Well, for starters there was a very old antique album, a recording of the Stabat Mater, do you know anything about that?"

Donald stared crossly at Jody, jaw clinched. "I was hoping we could keep this relationship of ours more business than personal."

"I'm sorry, Donald. I..."

"Do you know what I do, Jody?" The bearded man reached for another slice of bread from the basket.

"You're an architect."

"Yes." He carefully buttered one side with the precision of a surgeon. "I like to build things, Jody." He took a carefully measured bite and savored it as he swallowed. "The laws of physics, everyone knows them... well, almost everyone. They're concrete, provable, finite, and tangible."

The bearded man stared listlessly over Jody's shoulder, peering into the far-off shores of a distant nirvana. "It makes my work predictable, even to the layman." Another bite passed his lips, and his face grew dark and sullen. "You are coming to learn, not everything in this world is like physics; unpredictable, unseen, but always there, just under the surface of everything you touch."

"I'm sorry..."

Donald stopped him with a raised palm. "Please, no need to apologize." He settled back into a more comfortable posture. "The...uncertainties of life are everywhere, Jody. I can't expect to hide from them forever, any more than you can." He straightened his napkin and collected himself with a giant heaving sigh. "So...what is it?" He leaned in and stared down Jody intensely, eye to eye. "Tell me more about the Stabat Mater."

Jody weaved a meandering tale, recounting the strange events at The Study Hall, and his observations of the melancholy album that now haunted his dreams. He ended his speech and waited expectantly for a reply. "Do you know anything... anything at all?"

Donald's upper lip quivered. He dug deep into his back pocket and hastily riffled through it. "I can't... I thought I could, but I can't, not now." He threw down three well pressed hundred-dollar bills onto the table and took five steps toward the door. He stopped. Straightened the lapel of his jacket and returned to his seat. "I must apologize for my behavior."

"No apology needed, Mr. Longworth." The oddity of this man was growing exponentially, but Jody could little afford to offend such a valuable asset. He wanted answers about what the strange bearded man knew, but he needed his continued patronage more.

"Just call me Don, please."

"Sir? I mean, Don... sir? What's wrong?"

"Absolutely nothing." His face contorted and, just for a moment, the golden sparkle flitted from his eyes. Gingerly, he sat back down, replacing his cloth napkin on his lap, neatly folded, before participating in the meal with shaking hands.

Jody was perplexed. The man before him, fondling his bread, trying to eat his meal with dignity, was hiding something. He had come through too much to let such gaping question marks go unaddressed.

"What do you know?"

Donald closed his eyes, bowed his head, and ran the handle of his fork in tight concentric circles on the stark white tablecloth. "Jody, I haven't been completely honest with you."

The bearded man forced himself to stop his mindless dithering, cleared his throat, and very intentionally placed the fork down onto his plate. "Allen Tipton wasn't a good friend of mine. He couldn't stand the sight of me and did business with me as infrequently as possible."

Donald's piercing eyes met Jody's squarely. "Allen Tipton was my brother, my adopted brother, to be more precise. I was welcomed into the Tipton home shortly after the death of his younger sibling."

He paused and took a deeply drawn breath, resolving to say his peace in spite of an obvious desire to run away, evident in every twitch and mannerism he manifested in his uncomfortable wooden chair. "I know things about him, hard things, deep things, the kind of things that can break people. Do you know the kind of things I'm talking about?"

Jody knew exactly the kind of things he was talking about. He couldn't bring himself to speak just yet but nodded his understanding. A windless chill ran up Jody's spine.

"I've felt this before." Don shrank back in his chair, shoulders tensing, eyes clinched tightly. "Do you feel it?"

Jody nodded again, mouth agape.

"It's vile, oppressive. I didn't notice it last time I was here. It usually doesn't follow me away from that shop. I haven't felt it like this in a long time."

Donald wiped beading sweat from his brow with his napkin. He leaned in close across the table and stared. "It didn't follow me here, Jody. It followed you."

"Are you with the Parapsychological Association?"

Don's face scrunched in disappointment. "Oh, dear child, what have you done?" The peculiar book collector gave Jody a fatherly stare, the likes of which he'd only ever seen from his old boss. "Have you?"

"Have I what?"

Don slumped. Frustration flared through the squelched undertones of his question. "Have you seen the boy?"

Jody nodded.

"So did Allen, all the time. Leave it alone, Jody. It's not what you think it is."

The peculiar man checked his watch and grimaced. He sat down his fork and rose for a second time. As he left, he paused to admonish Jody one last time. "Leave it alone. If you know what's good for you, please, just leave it."

"How am I supposed to...."

Donald's fist rapped the table, rattling the dishes, nearly causing Jody's wine to slosh from its glass. He strained through clinch teeth. All eyes in the room were now on them both. "This is not your battle to fight, Jody. It is mine."

Don straightened the lapel of his suit coat, chest heaving as he stood up straight. "If you meddle with this monster you have stumbled upon, Jody, it will kill you. It will eat your soul. Leave it."

EIGHTEEN

D eath had knocked at Jody's door in the past, but, in time, it had always passed him by. Its cruel hand had taken people from him, but he had not, until this moment, stopped to think about death's plan for him, personally. It did not spring up from the wings and swoop down to take him. It waited, lurking in the shadows around every corner.

Something, faceless, formless, wanted him dead, and that disturbed him. A signed death warrant sat invisibly on the desk beside him. He could feel it.

Questions, so familiar to the condemned, filled his every thought. What do you do when you know you are going to die? How do you count the days that come next, after that sentence has been declared? Is it a beginning, or is it an end? Do you count up, or do you count down?

By the end of his cup of coffee, Jody decided that it had best be treated like a beginning, a new birth. A terrible confrontation with death may come any moment, but the verdict had already been delivered. It wants him dead. He could count up from that day.

Today was day two.

He spent most of day two trying to forget about the little boy speaking Latin in the corner of the room. Karen had helped him forget quite nicely earlier in the morning, a gentle touch that soothed the fire in his mind, but as day turned to night, his flesh slipped away from the blessed distraction of her company and into reality of his daily duties. It was his turn to close.

Darkness fell across the city outside his storefront window. He busied himself and tried to forget about the thing hunting him from the shadows while working alongside Meg. It was a bittersweet effort.

"Why didn't you answer my calls the other night?" Her tone was sharp and prodding.

The question stung more than it had a right to. Meg was a vicious and dogged inquisitor. She flipped the sign in the window from "Open" to "Closed".

"What are you talking about?" Jody's stomach tensed as the question slipped out of his mouth. Playing dumb? Really? That's never going to work.

"I called you like ten times the other night and you didn't answer me one single time. That isn't like you."

Jody chose silence and focused on polishing the coffee bar to a waxy reflective finish. But the harder and more determined he put his hands to a task, the more he could feel her stare raking across the back of his neck.

"And Billy... you ghosted him too."

"I did not."

"You did. That's low Jody Howard. You've been changing."

"No, I haven't."

She stood directly in front of him, demanding his focus, refusing to allow him to flit about the room like this conversation didn't matter. "Don't think I haven't noticed you've started drinking again. I can smell the beer on you every morning. In the morning, Jody. Are you partying hard at night or just throwing back a few before you come in to work?"

Jody tried to protest. It was useless.

She put a hand up to her lips and started to sputter. With great effort, she managed to hold back tears. "I told you, Jody. I told you I wanted something normal. Do you know what I meant, Jody? Do you?"

He frowned back at her, drowning, sorrowing. His mind leapt in front of her words, giving them meaning before she even uttered them. He knew. He had it, that thing that had escaped him since childhood, that simple, loving acceptance, and he threw it away. He chose Karen instead. The realization caught in the back of his throat, choking back any half-hearted attempt to protest.

"I wanted you, Jody Howard." She beat out the rhythm of her last words with her finger jabbing into his chest. "I wanted a normal you. The you I knew before. Where did you go?"

He didn't know. He nodded his head. He had gone somewhere. It was a long and terrifying journey that started sometime this past year, when he realized that he was going to graduate and would have to face the emptiness that lay beyond the bounds of campus. There was no home left to go back to in Virginia. It was erased, washed away by the whisky poured down the gullet of a drunk driver nine years ago. Home, or whatever was left of it, was just that nightmare, dead memories lying in state continually all around him.

Had that been it? Was that the true source of fear that caused him to falter and push away any hope he had at true happiness?

Gently, but insistently, he pushed her way. He lied. "You don't know what you're talking about. I'm fine."

"You're not fine. You've never been fine, Jody, but that's okay. I just can't be with a Jody who stops trying."

He sat down and turned away. He didn't want to hear her. Graduation had nearly destroyed him. His PTSD was almost uncontrollable in the chaos that followed his time at UC. The darkness, the voice of the snake curled up in his brain, was ruining him, like it had before.

He thought, for one fleeting night, he was walking out of that darkness and into a new day of hope. He found it again, a hope he thought lost for years, on that purple bridge over the Ohio river, on the heels of that first kiss. Since that kiss, he hadn't broken down screaming and crying in a puddle on the floor. He took his first drink in years that night. It calmed him, took the edge off of everything. When he drank the world still didn't make since, but it didn't have to. The questions, the fears, the memories, all mattered less. The snake stayed silent.

Meg sniffled softly behind his back. "You promised Billy you wouldn't drink anymore after that night."

Jody glared back at her over his shoulder. That night was eons behind him. No one had spoken of it in his presence since Billy pulled the gun out of his hand and shoved him into the cab of his Toyota pickup truck. It was a secret, their secret.

"What did he tell you?" he snarled.

"Nothing, just that you promised him before you came to UC that you would never drink again. He said you guys did stupid stuff back then."

"Is that all he told you?"

"Yes."

"Meg, I'm begging you. Please, drop this. I'm fine. You drink, Billy drinks, lots of people drink and they don't have any problems."

"Other people didn't find themselves in Betty Ford before the age of 18." Her reply echoed off the walls. It stung Jody's ears, and they started to itch.

"What does she know?" Jody's thoughts hissed at him.

She wiped her forearm across her red and swollen eyes. "You are in there, Jody. If you weren't in there somewhere, I wouldn't bother doing this right now." She drew in close again.

"You are a compassionate, loving, caring man, with a heart so big. You are beautiful in there."

Her hand fell gently on his chest. "I'm not afraid of you, Jody. I'm not afraid of this... mess you're dealing with." He couldn't bear to look her in the eye but it didn't stop her. "But I need to know that you will start trying again."

Deep pools in Meg's eyes pulled at Jody's heart. His jaw began to quiver. For a fraction of a second, the sternness in her countenance cracked and they connected, one hurting person to another.

The old brass ringer chimed and stepped between them, severing that very human moment when soul touches soul. "Hello there!"

"Karen," Jody choked. "You made it!"

She walked in with a short black sequence dress that made her toned thighs look a thousand miles long, grabbed his hand and placed her forehead against him. "I missed you."

She gave him a deep and passionate kiss conveying her longing so perfectly that Meg was compelled to divert her gaze. "Are you done here?"

"I think so." He looked sheepishly over at Meg. "You think you can finish up and lock..."

"I'll lock up on my way out, yeah." She didn't acknowledge Karen, or bother to tell them goodbye.

CHAPTER
NINETEEN

"I don't have to push him, just let me nudge him." Meg pleaded.

Billy lay back in his chair as far as permitted by the laws of physics, with his worn red and black Nikes propped up on the table. Rumbling snores rolled in uneven intervals from his vibrating lips and nose.

Jody clucked disapprovingly, though he couldn't help crack a smile. "You know, Meg, you ride him all the time about being immature. The way I see it..."

"Nope, no, uh uh," she raised her hand to Jody's face. "Talk to the hand." Meg rose from her seat with a single violent heave and went back to the coffee pot to freshen up her tepid cup.

Karen snickered. "I agree, he acts like he's in the eighth grade, tops."

Meg huffed as she poured steaming, dark liquid into her cup. In Meg's mind, Karen had no right to say anything about Billy, not here, not in this place.

Looking over the rim of her mug, she saw Karen's bare foot dangling dangerously close to Jody's knee, her leather sandals setting neatly, empty beneath her shapely legs under the table. Karen's bare toe touched Jody's leg and he didn't shrink away.

It aggravated Meg, infuriated her. Karen hadn't earned the right to cross into this sacred space, into the peace and refuge afforded their exclusive club, the closers. Karen was an inter-loper, only there by the express invitation of Jody, her boss, her Jody. As far as Meg could tell, Karen added nothing to this whole situation but a pretty face and firm body for Jody to cozy up to as they waited.

Jody whispered something into Karen's ear, and she laughed quietly. Her shy demeanor, her brightly flashing smile represented everything Meg wished she was, but feared she could never become. Karen left a delicate imprint of rouge lipstick on the rim of her mug and whispered discretely in reply behind an upturned palm.

Meg dropped her own arm with a thud. "Stop it. Please."

Jody gave her a cross look, as if he were completely unaware of the wrenching turmoil brewing deep inside her.

Billy jerked awake with a snort, nearly losing his balance rocking for a moment with flailing arms like a acrobat in peril high upon the tightrope. "Wh-what did I miss?"

Meg's scoffed, mumbling something about a loser.

The chimes on the door rang out, declaring the entry of the remaining supplicants for that night's vigil into the realms of the unknown. A rush of people poured into the room, starting a flurry of activity.

"Mr. Howard, thank you so much for accommodating our... non-traditional scheduling needs." Professor Austin marched in, her black hair and white dress flowing like an ethereal train behind her.

Billy collected himself. "Professor, good to see you."

She smiled and nodded in his direction. "Mr. Johnston, I didn't recognize you there... awake."

"Professor..." Jody tried not to laugh at the joke so master-fully quipped at his friend.

Meg snatched her mug and moved quickly back toward the

familiarity of the counter, being sure to give Karen as wide a birth as possible.

Jody watched her with a suspicious eye as he continued. "I don't think you told me what exactly you teach when we met last."

"Abnormal Psychology."

"That explains a lot," Meg grumbled.

"Karen, so glad to see you already here and settled in." She extended an ivory hand which the young woman rushed to embrace.

"Settled in?...You mean...you guys know each other?" Jody couldn't believe his ears, or eyes.

"Yeah, Dude, Karen's like numero uno on the sensitive scale around here. She brought me on after we landed on campus, taught me everything I know." Billy gave Professor Austin a nod and a fist bump.

"So you, know each other too." Jody pointed wildly back and forth between them.

"Dude, keep up." Billy patted him on the back as he moved about greeting his compatriots from the Parapsychological Association.

"We should be able to begin soon." Ms. Austin's voice was full of energy, more cheerful than just a few days ago. Her smile beamed unnaturally wide, almost Cheshire-like in its cartoonish perception. It made Meg sick to her stomach. It was some unfortunate trick of the evening lighting against her fair skin and dark lip color, but it didn't make it any less creepy. "It will only be a moment before the rest of our members join us."

"The rest?" The words blurted from Meg's mouth before she could pull them back in.

Words were tricky things and sometimes hard to control for her, especially in situations that made her nervous. She frankly didn't know if she could handle any more eccentric characters entering this already foreign situation, and hoped the parade of peculiars would come to an end sooner rather than later.

Before Ms. Austin could explain, a muscular young man burst through the front door, butt first. He was hunched over a cardboard box, yawning at the seams under the bulging mass of technological hardware jammed inside. He guided the large container over to the table where everyone had gathered and sat it down with a thud.

"Excuse me folks." He was winded from effort, but quite cordial.

Surprise washed over Meg. This new person was normal. Not only was he normal, but he was handsome, a beautiful coif of blonde hair crowning a perfectly tan late twenty something body. His handsome physique nearly made her forget her agitation toward Karen, nearly but not quite.

"Hi, I'm Chip Morris," he waived sheepishly to the assembly. "I'm the, um, tech guy I guess you could say, and these are the tools of the trade."

With a strong hand and learned eye, he plunged his arm deep into the box and began to pull out a menagerie of technical electronic implements that he organized on the table in the midst of the gathering. "Some of these things probably look a little familiar to you. You can look, but please don't touch. These beauties...". He pointed out a series of four different items that looked like camcorders. "...are motion sensing night vision and u.v. cameras. They are going to be our eyes in the dark. They could give us some kind of visual proof of a haunting if one truly is going on here."

Karen nodded politely. "I don't need a video to know what I feel."

Chip picked up a black box about the size of a cell phone and an array of multicolored lines across the top. "This is the classic K2 meter. We'll use several of these tonight. Basically, they pick up electromagnetic fields, which may indicate spiritual activity in the area."

He handed the K2 to Meg for her examination. She flipped it over clumsily in her fingers. "Don't worry, you're not going to hurt it. He reached down and flipped it on. The lights flashed to life and settled on the cool end of the spectrum. "The more red those lights get, the hotter the area is with spectral activity."

He picked up another, larger black box that looked like some sort of radio scanner. "And this beauty is the Spirit Box SB11. It allows spirits to communicate with us by manipulating radio frequencies as it does rapid scans through the spectrum."

"Like Bumblebee?" Billy asked, trying to compartmentalize the technology.

Chip laughed. "Yeah, if you're a Transformers fan, almost exactly like Bumblebee."

Two more technicians started helping Chip set up technology all over the shop. They sat up and ran wires for cameras to try to catch a view of as much square footage as possible. Everything was tied into some kind of master monitoring station and connected through Chip's laptop.

"And that's it. Okay, now this is the mothership." He held up his closed sleek, grey Apple laptop like a prized treasure of old. "All of this will be communicating to me through my trusty laptop here. I'll be stationed out in our van parked across the street. If you need to talk to me, just use these." He handed tiny walkie talkies to everyone. "Chanel 10, only 10, remember that. And one last thing...". Chip reached into a black backpack and pulled out what looked like a large iphone and a tiny microphone attachment. "You get to hold the new baby." He handed it to Billy with a flare of joyful fanfare, who received the item with bubbling elation.

"This is it?" Billy asked, jogging in place with excitement.

"That's it, my friend, fresh out of my personal basement lab of ghost hunting gadgets." Chip took a small bow for Billy's benefit. "I call it the Ghost-later...get it...ghost and translator." The rest of the room offered no reaction, but Billy was still on cloud 9.

"The word on the street is you guys have a little Latin-only speaker hiding in your rafters. This is basically a hand held computer set to google translate Latin to English based on vocal input. If the sounds the little... um, apparition, is making are actually being produced in the physical realm, and not by some kind of psychic telekinesis, this little gadget will pick it up through the mic and spit out a verbal translation through its speakers."

He could tell the profundity of this development was still going over the heads of his audience. "Like this see... E pluribus unum."

The box lit up with a green indicator in Billy's hand, and a female computerized voice reported the translation. "Out of many, one."

"Sweet," Billy smiled and admired the new tool like a brand new toy on Christmas Morning.

Ms. Austin rose from her seat with a slow and deliberate pace that denoted ceremony and demanded attention. "Thank you all for your cooperation. I understand these are trying times for everyone. Chip has just prepared our area of investigation tonight with a lot of technology and equipped us with tools of the trade that can bring clarity to the situation at hand and preserve evidence of the paranormal for those who may be of a more skeptical nature. But when I came here a few days ago, I could tell right away that something was wrong here, very wrong. I have never felt such an obvious and heavy malevolent presence in my ten years of doing local investigations. This is serious."

She raised her eyes and drew a great halted breath as if she was about to move on but suddenly froze in thought. "...And, I almost forgot." She chuckled. "These formal sessions can be tricky things. We could spend all night and find nothing, or we may have one of the most harrowing nights of our lives. Please, remember, ghosts are beings of emotions and infinite patience. They can lurk unseen, unfelt, and see things we don't want seen, even peer into our innermost thoughts and pry like a surgeon with a probe through our emotional memories. Be careful, guard your thoughts, guard your hearts. They can find your weakest, darkest moments and use them against you."

Jody gulped.

"That's always encouraging, huh." Billy chuckled grimly. "Just remember, take it serious bro. This is no joke."

The Parapsychological members divided themselves into groups and some paired off with the unprofessional and relatively unexperienced attendees assembled by Jody. Each group claimed their share of the paranormal detection equipment and combed the store. They covered every inch of the small shop in short order, asking questions, listening intently and, in the words of Billy "being open to the vibrations of the universe." All of their searching and questioning in the dimly lit corners of the Study Hall turned up nothing.

"Why is it hiding?" Ms. Austin clinched her teeth. "It didn't hide from me before." She returned again to each corner of the room, searching, becoming almost frantic. "Why are you hiding from me?"

Billy saw her flitting about and tried to get her attention. "Professor...Professor, are you okay? You might want to take a breath. You're starting to scare the children." He raised his walkie talkie to his mouth. "Chip, anything at all yet on the infrared?"

"Negative, nothing unusual on motion sensors, infrared, no emf spikes, we are still stone cold." Chip's voice squawked back.

Jody paced nervously. Something deep inside of him wanted to be validated, needed someone official to tell him that he hadn't led all of the people he loved down some insane rabbit hole of self-deception. This need for validation was even stronger than his desire to keep everything hidden in his past locked away from the prying eyes of anyone that had not already been given his complete confidence, that especially included the undead.

"There is one thing we could be missing." Jody disappeared through the painted door back into the area labeled Employees Only and emerged quickly again, followed by the sounds of the Stabat Mater.

"Woah, woah, what is that?" Chip's voice came through their walkies.

Jody pressed his talk key and explained to the group. "Things always seem to happen when I'm playing this record. It was one of Mr. Tipton's favorites."

"Is that it?" Ms. Austin called into the night with a blank, searching stare. "Do you like this music?"

The song rolled ominously off of the vinyl disk and through every nook and cranny. Ms. Austin took a deep breath in through her nostrils. "Mmmm, feel that? It's building, isn't it?"

"Who's in the back room?" The excitement in Chip's voice was clear even over the static on the airway.

Billy took quick account and replied. "Um, no one Chip. We're all in the front room at this moment."

"I've got a clear heat signature on the U.V. camera in the back room. It just walked past the record player. It's moving slowly, like it's looking for something."

Karen interwove her cold fingers with Jody's and squeezed him tightly. "Please don't. Please don't. Please don't."

All of their K2 meters spiked red and squealed at once. Karen dropped her's with a gasp, and it spun violently on the ground.

"Are you getting this, Chip," Billy asked behind a shaking walkie talkie.

"Every bit. That thing in the room is... no way... guys the

door there just went cold. I mean blue cold. There's a hand-print! I see a warm hand on the door."

All eyes rested on the painted door. No one moved, save to tremble. No one breathed.

The doorknob did not move, but the door swung slowly open. The creaking on the old hinges sent chills down Jody's spine. Through the darkened doorway walked a little boy, dressed in knickers and a cap, like someone out of the 1930's. He passed in front of a bookcase. The fabric of his body flickered.

At points he seemed solid and the next moment, transparent, the books behind him clearly visible. The boy walked straight forward, never once looking left or right, toward Jody and Karen. He knelt at their feet and picked up the spinning K2 meter. He stood and looked Karen in the eye. With a mischievous grin, opened his mouth and a loud squeal just like the K2 meter came from his throat. It shook her, she fell back against the bookcase and cowered behind Jody, quaking.

"What do you want?" Ms. Austin raised her voice so she could be clearly heard over the devices. "Tell us. How can we help you?"

The boy's head snapped unnaturally fast to the right to face the black-haired woman. He shut his mouth and all of the K2 meters went black and dead silent.

"What are you wanting to tell us?" Ms. Austin repeated, keeping her tone steady and calm.

The boy's mouth moved, but the sounds came from the squealing speakers of the Spirit Box. "Stabat mater dolorosa juxta crucem lacrymosa." He walked slowly toward Ms. Austin and held out his arms, palms open and extended, his face cold, angry, annoyed. "Dum pendebat Filius." The ghost-later responded. "The grieving Mother stood weeping beside the cross where her Son was hanging." He dropped his arms and lowered his chin, staring at her through thinning angry slits of eyelids. He walked toward her, taking labored but still childlike breaths echoing through the Spirit Box.

"No, no, no no no. You can't." Ms. Austin protested. "I won't let you. No!" She visibly shook in fear. "You can't. I don't allow it! No!"

He extended a tiny index finger and lightly touched her stomach. The raven-haired psychic grasped at her gut and moaned in a mournful and sad groaning. She heaved and groaned louder and louder, then fell to her knees weeping, hot tears streaming down her face.

In a flash, the boy stood before Jody again. His mouth moved but the voice groaned through Ms. Austin's throat. "Quis est homo qui non fleret Matri Christi si vederet in tanto supplicio?" The translation came back from the green flashing box. "Who is the person who would not weep seeing the Mother of Christ in such agony?"

His image flashed and he appeared before Meg. "Quis est homo?" It flashed again. "Who is the person?", then before Billy "Quis est homo?" Then before Jody, but leaning down and peering around Jody's legs as if a child peeking beneath a table, the specter looked deep into Karen's eyes and repeated. "Quis est homo?" She screamed. The child scooted back and rose. The mischievous smile returned, and he rose an arm toward Jody as if lifting a gun. "Quis est homo?" "Who is the person?", the translator asked one final time.

The phantom boy flickered and vanished. Billy ran into the back room and lifted the undulating needle from the old record with a crunch and flicked off the turntable.

"Is everybody okay?" he called from the dark room. "Professor? Professor?" He burst back in. "Somebody help Ms. Austin." Billy scooped her into his arms and looked up at Jody with grave concern. "What did we do?"

Professor Austin, lay in his arms, twitching and mumbling, "Who is the person...who is the person...weep...agony."

TWENTY

I t was day 5, since the death threat from the great beyond awakened his sense of impending doom and mortality. Jody quietly rocked in his desk chair, listening to metal scraping against metal, wondering where the sounds came from, wondering what they meant, wondering when the terrible words uttered from the strange little boy would come for him and change his life forever, instead of just the professor's.

The door creaked and the strong but aged figure of his expected visitor darkened lintel and post. "Mr. Howard, thank you for allowing me back into your office this evening. Trust me, I understand how valuable time away from the office can be and I'm sorry to deprive you of yours. And..." He cleared his throat awkwardly.

"I'm always glad to do business with you, Don." Jody pulled a small box from a stack beside his computer. "Any time. The meal was delicious. Thank you for paying for it."

The onetime book clerk took out his pocketknife and gingerly worked the seal of the box. "I'm just going to be extra careful here."

He reached in the parcel and pulled out an experienced and

beautiful tome. The cover was leather stained black, a patina of deep rich brown showing through its aged surfaces. Deep ornamental carving and flourishing embossing adorned the cover. In the center panel, amidst a carefully fashioned floral spray the title was clearly set, *Holy Bible*. "A rare 1869 original William W. Harding Bible."

"Wow," a smile grew across Don's bearded face. He reached out with careful anticipation to hold the book, like a father awaiting his newborn son. "It is magnificent." Carefully, he thumbed the pages. "Precious, so very precious."

Jody smiled politely. After enduring such harrowing experiences, the bloom was somewhat off the rose of the antique book business. "It does look beautiful."

The collector looked up from his breathless examination. His countenance fell. "Something's wrong."

"Sir? I mean, Don... sir? What's wrong with the book."

"Absolutely nothing. I will take it, but I was hoping to give you a straight answer to your question." His eyes narrowed and he took a glancing peek over his shoulder. "I do know something, about the Stabat Mater, about this whole situation. I know a few things."

Jody was perplexed. The man before him, who until moments ago was fondling the cover of an old book the way schoolboys do bags of candy, had turned on his proverbial heel. Before him stood a fount of wisdom and knowledge, the kind of wisdom and knowledge that could change his life forever. He had come through too much to let such gaping question marks go unaddressed.

"What do you know?"

Donald closed his eyes, bowed his head, "The boy is part of my past, and Allen's...a story as intertwined as the fabric of our very beings." The old man sat down the Bible very carefully and stared sullenly at Jody. "We were brothers, together once, in this old townhouse you now call a coffee shop. I always felt like one of them, a natural member of their family. That's why I came back here all those years, all the time, first for Allen, now for you. It's because this… is home. What happens here means… it just means more to me."

Jody wasn't sure what the bearded man meant, but he knew behind those strange sparkling eyes were answers yet unperceived. "Your brother? The little ghost boy, is he…your brother? Mr. Tipton?" Jody could hardly believe his ears. "What's the boy trying to say? Why won't he leave us alone? What does the record have to do with anything?"

The old man raised his hand. "In good time, all in good time."

He pulled up a chair and sat down heavily, his shoulders carrying an invisible burden that had held him down for years. "It takes time to unlock so many old chains and unwind their serpentine tails." He pulled a tightly rolled Cuban cigar from the inside breast pocket, expertly trimmed it and lit it with a match he struck against Jody's old work bench. He offered it to Jody who politely declined.

"Hm, just as well," he coughed, "terrible habit." He sucked down the grey smoke of the brown tobacco and chewed it over and over in his teeth.

"This… is the flavor of my youth. My adopted father smoked at least one of these right here in our living room every day until he passed away. God rest his soul." He admired the cigar as he rolled it between his fingers against the yellowing light from the overhead lamp.

"You mean Allen's father?"

"No, after Allen's father died, his mother remarried. They wanted a child together but… well… it doesn't much matter. I was around a lot, didn't have a place and family of my own. So, they adopted me. He still passed away when we were all very young, a heart attack I believe. He gave each of us something to remember him by. He left Allen a collection of records, myself a love for fine tobacco, and our poor mother... he left memories of a happy life, twice broken by death. The heartbreak nearly killed her. Being a single mother is hard, but back then... it was soul crushing. She did the best she could trying to raise three boys and run a business, desperately fighting to keep his memory alive... but it finally broke her. She fell into a depression and would fly into maniacal tantrums with me and my brothers over the slightest little things."

He cleared his throat. His voice crackled and Jody could see him holding back tears. "Truth be told, she used to beat us half to death over the slightest little thing, me, Allen, all of us. There was no end to it, once she got started. One morning Peter knocked over her favorite perfume bottle, lavender oil, and broke it. Glass and oil went everywhere, the stink was overwhelming. I tried to clean it up but mom knew what happened right away. She grabbed Peter by the hair of the head and started beating him against the edge of the nightstand. Over, and over, she slammed his head into that little table and cursed him with every breath. I was crying, pleading trying to get her to stop. She slapped me down with the back of her hand right across my jaw. Allen just balled up in the corner crying into his nightshirt. There was nothing he could do, nothing either of us could do. Peter was dead long before she stopped. She let go of his hair and he just laid there, looking at me with those dull glazed eyes."

"I'm so, sorry..."

"She made us tell everyone he fell off the roof, that we snuck up there after breakfast and were playing too close to the edge and he fell off the roof."

The old man sobbed and coughed and struggled to regain his composure. "Afterwards, Allen used to get up every day and put on that record. He'd sit in the floor and play, talking to himself the whole time. He wouldn't say a word to me or mom. He'd just play and talk, and then he'd turn off the record and not a peep for the rest of the day. Finally, I cornered him, asked him what he was doing, why he wouldn't answer me. I tried to turn off the record and he screamed just as loud as he could scream. He said I couldn't turn off the album because Peter liked it and Peter would only play with him while the album was playing." The bald and bearded man sobbed, broken, elbows on knees, face to the earth.

Jody quickly gathered tissues and a bottle of water which he dutifully offered. Donald thanked him, unscrewed the cap and took an awkward swig, splashing glistening droplets of water down his still black beard. It seemed odd that such strong and calloused hands, once used to construction, should now falter at the weight of a water bottle.

"Thank you." The man righted himself.

Honesty was a quality Jody greatly admired. Perhaps it was because he had so much in his past, he preferred to not be honest about. His own secrets were best kept close and silent, but before him sat a paragon of honesty and openness, the likes of which Jody had never seen before, and it garnered great respect.

Jody leaned in earnestly with furrowed brow and down-turned expression. The bearded man's words were heavy, dizzyingly so. He breathed in a deep ragged breath. It was more information than he had hoped to glean in one day. It bulged and stretched inside his soul, causing his stomach to churn like a meal far too well enjoyed.

"That is a lot to unpack Donald. I can't believe you had to..."

"There is more." Donald drank again. "One night, I came downstairs. I had heard a commotion. I could tell something had happened with Allen and I wanted to help him take care of it before mother found out. As I descended the stairs, I could see Allen in the corner covered in blood. The Stabat Mater was blaring loudly from the record player. I leapt over the last few steps to get to him and when I landed, on the floor in front of him, I saw our mother. Her head was smashed into an unrecognizable pulp from the baseball bat he was holding. 'Peter told me I could do it.' he said."

Jody gasped.

"I cleaned it all up, all of it." He choked again. "I drug her body out into the alley, and positioned it a little. Allen never said much about it, but I had to... I had to cover what had been done. I told everyone over and over again that she couldn't take it. She had gone insane with grief over father and Peter and had leapt to her death."

He steadied himself and finally spoke without a weak and quivering voice. "We were separated after that. He went with one set of relatives and I with another. When he grew up, he ended up taking the house. I told them I wanted nothing to do with it. Then, thirty years ago, he called me. I could hear the same album playing in the background. He said Peter had something he wanted to say to me. I hung up the phone. It was the last straw. I couldn't do it anymore. He would barely speak to me after that, never forgave me for leaving him and Peter alone."

Jody stood up and backed away from the desk, fixated on the faded purple record cover. "*The grieving mother stood weeping beside the cross where her son was hanging.* It's about your mother, grieving over Peter's Death. That is horrible. I think I'm going to be sick." He leaned over one of the nearby wastebaskets.

"And it's about Peter, getting his revenge."

"But why you... and me... now, I mean still... There's something about this whole thing, it really does tie us all together. You... me... Peter."

"What is it?"

The old man just shook his head.

CHAPTER
TWENTY-ONE

Meg squeezed into the same tight black party dress she wore to Mr. Tipton's funeral. It was the best dress she owned, the only one really. Carefully, with a steady and learned hand she put on her makeup and eyeshadow, outlined her lashes and added just a dash of sparkle to shimmer on her cheeks. She puckered her lips and worked in her red lipstick as she examined her handiwork.

Minutes later, black sequin clutch in hand, she stepped out of a Yellow Cab onto the sidewalk in beautiful Mt. Adams, just in time to see the picturesque sunset blaze across the sky in orange, blues, and yellows above the Cincinnati skyline.

Before she could even step through the doorway of the club, music was seeding life into the evening air, bleeding through window, door, and mortar.

"No, I said the Pavilion, Pa-vil-ion. Yeah, right. Yes, I'm already here." She hung up the little grey phone and tucked it safely into her clutch.

Meg thought she had explained the entire plan to Missy before she left work that evening, but obviously not clearly enough. Missy was halfway across town at another night club she frequented, or more precisely, where a guy she frequented worked as bar tender.

She had lost her wingman, as it were, and found herself at a distinct disadvantage. To Meg, Missy represented life outside of The Study Hall. Missy was a friend she could trust, that didn't have ulterior motives and had no designs what-so-ever on her pants or what was in them. She was fun, always down to party, and most importantly never smelled like coffee.

Crossing over the threshold, the black door of the club was swung open for her by a sharply dressed boulder of a man with a handsome smile. She drank in the wash of sound and lights that greeted her. It was time to cut loose, with or without her best friend.

Bodies jumped and twirled, sloshing drinks held high in red solo cups. Lights bounced frantically to the rhythm of the music doled out by a bobbing headphone-clad disc jockey. The night was warm, the atmosphere inviting, begging her to take part and lose her sorrows and fears in the sea of skin, celebrating night and life.

Still, she dared not venture out amongst the press of dancing bodies on the outdoor patio without Missy. Too much would be left to chance without someone to help her navigate the pitfalls of her delicately fashioned plan. Tonight, she was going to have the time of her life and meet the man of her dreams. She didn't know who he was yet, but she could feel it in her bones. If he was going to be anywhere in the universe, it had to be here, and it had to be tonight.

Everything had to go perfectly. She had to look perfect. She had to dance perfect. She had to smile, perfectly. When left to her own devices, she was prone to wild and unbridled gyrations under the influence of an 808 drum and one too many umbrella drinks. That is why Missy was such an important part of the plan. Without proper supervision, she would never be able to pull this off. So, she nestled into the elegantly curved bar inside the room labeled "The Penthouse" in neon red letters under a stylized blue angled roof. She deftly flashed her id, ordered an amaretto sour, and turned to watch the room while she sipped at her enticingly sweet concoction. It was only one drink, just enough to take the edge off until her friend got there.

That is how Missy found her when she finally arrived, leaning back, elbows propped on the curved bar sipping what was, by then, her fifth amaretto sour.

"Oh, dear Lord, Meg!" She caught herself almost yelling across the room. "Meg...honey..." She sidled up to her friend, taking an empty barstool. "How are you doing?" Her voice was chipper, but she could already tell tonight was going to be a disaster.

"I'm fine, just fine, we're all fine here. How are you?" Meg's words slurred together a bit and her eyes swam freely around the room as she talked.

Missy lovingly put her arm around Meg's swaying shoulder. "Okay honey, it's time to go."

"Nope, nope, nope." Her reply bubbled up from somewhere deep inside her well-malted stomach. "I can't. I have to do this."

She pulled Missy's nose within an inch of her own and stared uncomfortably at her eyeball to eyeball. "I *have* to do this. It's almost too late... too late. Do you know what that means? Almost, not enough time left. I have to have time left. I have to do this!"

"Okay, okay. I'm sure you've got plenty of time, all the time in the world."

"No!" She immediately modified her voice from a yell to a whisper. "Listen to me... I like, nope, nope, nope... I'm in lo-ooove," her declaration was interrupted by an involuntary burp, "Jody Howard."

"Who?"

"You, know whooo... Jody, from the shoffy cop... the coffee shop."

"Oh, yes," Missy nodded in agreement though she barely remembered her mentioning him and she could really care less.

"He's already there, in the, at the, you know, with some other girl."

"No, no I don't girl. At the what?"

Meg could tell she was clearly not getting her point across, so she started miming along with her explanation. "The bed, with the bow chicka wow wow."

Missy immediately jumped off her stool and grabbed Meg by the hand. "Yep, time to go."

Meg dug her heels into the ground and pulled hard against her friend's urging. "Nope. I am not time to go yet."

"Oh, I think you are."

"Just, give me a second." Meg pulled away from Missy's grip. "I'm going to be fine." For a moment, she looked more like a five-year-old throwing a temper tantrum than a beautiful young lady. Missy took a breath and let speak her peace.

"I don't need to go yet. I just need...some time. I need some time, and food." She rubbed at her churning stomach.

Missy knew food on a drunken tummy is rarely a good idea, but just as unappealing was a retching hungry drunk dry heaving beside her for the rest of the night. She gave in to her friend's request. They placed a food order at the bar and told the bartender they would be sitting out on the balcony. Missy offered her arm to steady Meg on their journey through the Penthouse and out into the night air.

It was a beautiful night and the balcony at The Pavilion provided an excellent view of the city from its perch high above one of Cincinnati's seven hills. The panoramic view of the city's skyline took their breath away. The colorful tiara crowning the Great American tower glistened over the humming metropolis. It was distant but somehow almost seemed close enough to reach out and touch.

Halfway through their appetizer, Meg reached her hand to

point out the beautiful image to Missy, when she was stopped cold. She slurred something about thinking she saw Jody over there...or it could have been something about his underwear, it was hard to tell, but Missy didn't want to risk any kind of chance meeting with this Jody person tonight.

"You know what, Meg, I'm not really that hungry. Let's just go get a cab. We'll have you home in no time." One look at Meg's downturned features revealed it was too late.

Seated at a tiny table for two in the corner of the balcony, perfectly outlined by the lights of the urban sprawl, were Jody and Karen, engaged in pleasant conversation, and sharing tastes of one another's plates between laughs and coy batting eyelashes. Nothing happened for a moment. Missy had the faintest glimmer of hope. Perhaps the worst was over. Perhaps, just perhaps, they would be able to turn around, walk quietly to the sidewalk and she could pick up the pieces as Meg poured out her soul behind the back of some poor unsuspecting cabby. Then, Jody leaned over the main course and kissed Karen so sweetly, so tenderly, even Missy's toes curled in her tight heels.

"That's it. That is just about all I can..." Meg marched, with more clarity of purpose and determination than she had felt all night, up to their table and drug bumbling Missy sputtering and objecting behind her. Clearly, the unwitting lovebirds were caught off guard by Meg's appearance. Jody lost balance at the very sight of her and nearly fell out of his chair when she stomped up beside them with a chiseled, raging scowl.

"Oh, hi, Meg," he stammered, righting himself.

Missy was afraid to take one step further. She stayed far enough away not to get caught in the explosion if anything went down, but at the same time she had to be close enough to observe everything. She was her ride or die, she just hoped that it was more of the former and less of the later tonight.

Meg did not speak, not one word. Her lip trembled. Her arms crossed, face turned red and eyes welled atop giant puffy bags of pitiful, pouty emotion. The two lovers, staring questioningly at one another, were a vision more painful than verbal lashing, a pure expression of deep hurt and disappointment. At long last she opened her mouth to form words and her warbling vocal cords choked them out.

"Jody, I just want to tell you something."

She reached down, took his drink from the table and splashed it violently in his face. She curtsied to Karen and replaced the glass from whence it came. She turned on her heels and marched with an air of determination back into the Penthouse with Missy in tow.

CHAPTER
TWENTY-TWO

"Something's wrong, I can tell." Jody pushed against the well-worn brass plate on the old wooden door and entered the Study Hall.

The familiar bell rang, and a man in a well pressed suit, bald head, and long perfectly trimmed black beard, bumped into them on his way out the door. He nearly knocked Karen over. "I'm so sorry, my dear." His voice, his beard and bright eyes were unmistakable.

Karen was quite embarrassed. "It's alright, Mr. Tipton... I mean, Mr. Longworth, sir. I should have been watching where I was going."

The old man smiled warmly. "It's good to see you, my dear." The smile fell from his face and he paused, as if looking for perfect words that would not come. "I'll see you again, soon. I know it. Good night, and good night to you as well, Jody." He continued on his way without another look.

"That guy is so... weird." Jody grabbed a dish towel and started dabbing at his dress shirt, still damp from Meg's assault. "I don't know why she did it. Maybe she just snapped. I know that had to be so embarrassing for you."

Karen folded her arms and waited on her boyfriend to stop

frantically trying to fix things long enough to have an actual conversation. He eventually got the hint and froze like a deer in the headlights. "There's something seriously wrong with her, Jody. I worry about you spending so much time with her around here. She's not stable. There's no telling what kind of ideas have gotten into her head."

"Ideas?"

Karen answered him with a scolding look.

Jody looked awkwardly about at his late evening clientele, hoping that he hadn't embarrassed her or himself. "Oh, come on, Karen. For all of her faults, Meg is one of my oldest friends in the world. Plus," Jody came around the counter and took Karen's reluctant hand. "She has made it abundantly clear that she's never wanted anything more."

"A chilled glass and an unexpected shower say otherwise. There is more there. You don't have to be psychic to see it."

"She is my friend, nothing more." Jody tried to reassure her, but he could tell from her continued sullenness that she would not be consoled. "What is actually on your mind?"

The beautiful and sad angel spread her wings wide behind her and lifted her face toward the heavens. "I had high hopes for tonight's dinner. It was going to be... special."

"More special than a public spectacle?" Jody shut up quickly, seeing she was not amused. Karen folded her wings once more and closed herself off, turning her face toward the window. "Oh come on, honey. I didn't mean it...I know you were serious, you had something important you wanted to say. What was it?"

"It was perfect, the perfect moment, now it's ruined." Karen's eyes were beautiful, piercing. Even when she was disappointed and angry, they lit a fire deep inside him he never knew existed. "Not now, I can't now. I want it to be special."

The young man working behind the coffee bar shuffled past

them sheepishly. "Sir, if you don't mind, the last customer left a little while ago and I'm 20 minutes past my shift anyway."

"Oh, sure." Jody beckoned him to go on and told him not to worry, he would clean and lock up.

As the young man left, Karen brushed past Jody. "It is getting pretty late. I think I'll just head on home."

Jody deftly positioned himself between her and the door, leaned in, and turned on the charm. "Please, I can't take it. What were you going to tell me?"

Karen pursed her lips. "You will find out soon enough." She motioned as if to push on past him, but stopped. "Did you leave that on?"

The sound of orchestra and chorus rising to a crescendoed lamentation filtered into the bookstore from behind the door marked Employees Only. Whatever had happened, the last thing he wanted was to alarm Karen after everything else he had put her through that night. "Give me a sec. Make us some coffee and I'll go turn that thing off."

Karen smiled and twirled, her twinkling eyes shooting over her shoulder at him. Her coyness hid a quiet nagging concern. She stepped behind the bar, quickly measured grounds, poured water and turned on the percolator.

Jody casually opened the old painted door and turned on the light. He took one step toward the old record player. The door slammed forcefully behind him, rattling the door jam and causing the wooden planks beneath his feet to quake.

"Karen!" Jody immediately threw himself at the door and seized the old iron doorknob. It was ice cold. It would not turn, nor would the door yield as he pressed against it.

"Karen!" he cried again, taking a quick step back and throwing his shoulder against the immovable wood.

"Jody!" She ran toward the door to aide him but was stopped short. A specter like fog streamed from around a book-case and swirled into the form of an old woman in a long light-colored dress. Her eyes were hollow, deep, black holes, and her skin a thin, pallid veil laid over bone. The woman floated toward her, hovering just above the ground, for her feet had never materialized. As she came nearer, piercing cold eyes filled empty sockets and her flesh tightened and plumped until the solid image of an elderly woman stared back at her.

"Karen, I can't get out!" Jody screamed, still struggling with the door.

The old woman glared at Karen with contempt but said nothing. "Jody! Jody! Help me!" They were the only words she could force out of her body. She quaked, tears beginning to fall down her cheeks.

The ghost shook her head, never lifting her eyes from the young lady she held captivated by fear. The phantom turned her head agonizingly slowly to glance over her shoulder at the door where Jody was thrashing so desperately. In an instant, the hag lunged toward Karen stopping millimeters from her nose.

Karen instinctively recoiled. As she slunk back and tensed into a ball of abject fear, the old woman rose her hand and slapped Karen firmly across the face with an open hand. The force transferred from the ethereal hand snapped Karen's head to the side and forced her to the ground.

"No! Jody!" Helplessly Karen crawled across the floor, begging for assistance, refusing to open her eyes and look on her attacker.

The hair on her neck stood on end, as if she had strayed too close to a live wire. She felt a tendril of her hair rise up from her head. With a giant tug, she was yanked from the ground by the hair on her head and drug over to the counter. Karen struggled hard against the unseen hand. She planted her palms firmly against the countertop and pushed up with all her might, holding her head up off of the hard surface. The hag leaned in and tried to shove her face into the counter. Wave after wave of forceful thrusts rained down on her, an invisible hand pushing her over and over again.

"Stop! Stop!"

The old hag grabbed her by her shoulders and spun her around. She lunged in close once more, stinking breath washing over Karen's face from mere inches away. It smelled of sickeningly strong lavender. Her bony hand slid off Karen's shoulder and down to her waist. Fingernails scratched and dug into her skin as the phantasm's hand drew up under her blouse and bloodied her all the way to her stomach. It tilted its scowling face and pushed its fingers into Karen's skin, puncturing her stomach with five fingernail shaped slits around her belly button.

"No! Stop!" Karen howled in anguish. Her spirit broke within her as the ghostly fingers broke her skin.

"No! Please!" Her universe was consumed with sobs of sorrow. Muscles limp, she gave up her fight.

"I can't fight it! I can't keep it away anymore! I'm not strong enough!"

Jody remembered the record. He broke away from his battle with the immoveable door and yanked the record player from the old nightstand pulling its power cord free from the wall. The turntable ground to a halt and the music slurred to an unearthly and sinking silence. Jody ran back to the door. It opened easily, normally, at the slightest flick of his wrist against the knob.

He burst through the doorway and took Karen into his arms. She was crying uncontrollably, out of breath, hair disheveled. "What happened?"

Karen buried her head into his chest. "It hit me! It hit me, Jody. It hit me and it scratched me."

He stammered his words and cradling her face in his trembling hands lifted her gazed to him. "Oh, my God, Karen." Jody ran his finger softly over her cheek as she recoiled, her skin burning at his touch.

"I see it." A large red handprint emerged, emblazoned her face, every finger plainly visible.

Karen struggled to catch her breath between sobs. "It stabbed me in the stomach!"

He lifted her blouse and traced the bright red scratches from her side to her stomach. His hand immediately clasped at the bleeding punctures around her naval. They oozed blood but were shallow. He was able to stop the bleeding right away with the pressure of his palm.

As delicately as possible, he led her to the bathroom. The whir of the metallic ratcheting made her jump as he gathered a fist full of paper towels and then thrust them under a stream of cold water.

"Here, this may help the swelling." Delicately, he dabbed the wet paper against her cheek. He took more and dabbed at the scratches and the puncture wounds.

It cooled and soothed the burning, but Karen needed to know what happened, what the old woman had done to her body.

"Let me see," she protested, pushing aside his helping hand. The bright red handprint glowed beneath the cruel buzzing florescent lights. "It's her hand. She slapped me."

"Does it still hurt?"

"Yes. It all hurts."

"Here, let me get you some ice." Jody tried to leave, but Karen took his arm firmly in her hand and would not let go.

"You can't leave me here."

He nodded knowingly and gently took her hand. Together, they went back to the front room. Jody sat her at a table right in front of the counter and gathered ice from the freezer into a plastic baggie.

"Here."

Karen took the baggie and gingerly placed it on the handprint. "I don't understand, Jody. What was that?"

She had grown accustomed to the world around her making at least a certain amount of sense, even the supernatural had its own special rules of cause and effect. She couldn't quite figure this one out. The pain, the adrenaline, all conspired to keep her from putting the pieces together.

"It must be his mom?"

"Who's mom?"

"Peter...and Allen's mom. She did some pretty horrible things."

Karen's face reddened and she couldn't stop herself from crying. "It was terrible. Jody, this has to stop. I don't want to do this anymore. I can't do this anymore."

"Then let's finish it. Do it right now. What do you say?" He pulled his cellphone out of his jeans pocket and dialed seven quick numbers.

"No." Karen reached out and took the phone from him before he could press send. "I need to... tell... I need you... just you... I need to tell you...". Her gaze and her voice trailed off into the distance. "Oh my God... she knows."

"What? Tell me...what does she know?" Jody's soul reached out to her. She was in such pain. He just wanted to help her, console her.

"I'm pregnant."

Jody fell to his knees. He could barely breathe. All the world turned on those two words. Every priority changed, every thought, every concern. The world before those two words was entirely meaningless.

"I'm sorry. I'm so sorry." She sobbed into her hand.

Nothing about this was what she wanted. She wanted him to be happy to tell her they'd get through this together. Instead, he was kneeling in front of her touching her stomach, softly dabbing at her wounds, wanting to heal her and console her all at once.

"No, honey, no, there's nothing to be sorry about. I love you. I love you so much."

He gathered himself and pulled her gently to him. He held her softly, in that eerily quiet coffee shop, under the yellowing lights. "You are my world. Our child... is my world." He was going to protect his world. Nothing would stand in his way.

He guided her to on one of the couches in the front room, and knelt beside her, still tending her wounds, trying to soothe her and comfort her enough to allow her to rest. With blood-stained hands, he played with her hair and caressed her forehead, talking softly to her deep into the night until finally she found rest.

As she rested, he pulled out his cellphone and went to work indeed.

"Billy, yes, this is Jody. We have to do it now...No, we can't wait any longer. This thing just attacked Karen. Yes, there's blood everywhere. Get everyone together, at the store, now, the professor, the whole team. Yes, even Meg. We're not waiting 'til Sunday. Now...I don't care if you think it's a bad idea... yes... everyone."

CHAPTER
TWENTY-THREE

Professor Austin cleared her lungs of bad energies and pushed out negative thoughts and emotions with a deep breath. The grandfather clock tolled twice.

"It is time, we begin. Gather around the table. Find a seat and get comfortable. Is everybody ready? We need focus and attention. I do not want to give this thing any more power than it already has. Tonight, it leaves, once and for all, and we'll all be better for it."

Jody remembered Professor Austin's admonitions when she agreed to come on such short notice. She warned that she was still weak from their last encounter and Karen, her right hand and best assistant, was probably unable to withstand attack because of her compromised mental and emotional state. He could hear her warnings about energy and emotional vulnerability. He did not heed her well. He wanted this over and done, once and for all.

Karen was not ready. Her roughly bandaged wounds still stung. Her flesh rebelled against her will, trembling in spits and spurts. It was shock, or so she was told by the professor. She didn't want to be here, in this accursed coffee house, preparing to face down the most powerful and dark entity she had ever known. She told the professor that. She told Jody that. But, she had no choice.

Jody could not be free of this space or of the thing that hid inside it, he was bound to it, and probably could not leave without dragging that foul imp from hell with him. It must be dealt with, for Jody's sake, and for the sake of their unborn child.

"I can't find balance. I can't center myself like this," She whispered to Jody. He was seated between herself and Meg. "She's here. She's always here."

The professor leaned into the ear of her faithful assistant and whispered. "You are compromised. This thing is too much for you. You must regain objectivity and separate from your emotions."

Jody squeezed Karen's hand gently. "Honey, if you need to leave..."

"I am NOT running anymore." Her voice echoed off of the book lined walls. She paused, and continued speaking, more softly, voice still shaking. "No woman, man, or child, dead or alive is ever going to make me run, ever again. This place, this baby, you, are all too important. I am going to stay and I'm going to see this thing through to the end."

Meg gasped. All eyes turned to her and then slowly settled on the chattering couple clinging to one another.

"Seeing no objections, let us begin." Ms. Austin began an orientation about communication with the deceased.

"We are gathered in a circle because it represents the completeness of the flow of the universe, both physical and metaphysical. It is also a sign of unity and helps to focus our energies so that spirits we wish to communicate with can better use that energy to communicate with us. So, please, if you do not believe, suspend your unbelief. If you harbor hate, resentment, ill will of any kind toward anyone present here, please, release it, let it go. We must not harbor anything between us that can block that precious flow of energy. Do not let negative emotions rule you here. Release them as well. Close your eyes. Take in a deep breath, as deep of a breath as you can. Focus on the negative, the hate, the fear, the anger, the stress. Everything negative within yourself. Hold that breath. Ball that negative energy up in your chest, concentrate on it, draw it in from every corner of your body. When you breath out, you will release all of that energy with your breath. It will leave you. Ready? Breathe out."

The room hissed as everyone exhaled. "Feel the peace. Feel the openness."

Jody wasn't certain if he felt relaxed or exhausted. His heart fluttered in his chest. His body hummed with adrenaline from the insanity of the day. He felt empty, well, he wanted to be empty, but deep inside his emotions relentlessly clung to his earthly shell.

"Now take your hands and extend them slowly to the side. Take the hand of the person on either side of you. Hold them, feel them, feel the energy flow from fingertip to fingertip. Feel us become one. Keep your mind clear, release, flow."

He didn't understand it, but he thought that maybe, just maybe, something was happening. The hair on his arms began to rise and he felt a low charge of electricity flow over his skin in tiny waves. It was almost thrilling, startling for sure, but he pushed down his fear and tried to stay as open and calm minded as possible.

"Yes, yes, feel the spirit world opening. Remain calm, remain silent, and I will now attempt to contact the other side. Do not be afraid. The spirits can manifest in many ways, just be open, willing to hear their voices."

Jody breathed in deep and once again pushed down his fear and cleared his mind. He was determined to see this through, to tell the spirits they needed to crossover or whatever Ms. Austin said she could do for them.

"Hear us spirits. Our hearts are open. Draw near and speak to us." Silence. "Hear us spirits. Draw near to us. We wish to speak to you." Silence.

"Hear us spirits. Why do you remain here? We want to know." Silence. "Why do you stay here?" Professor Austin's voice grew louder. "Why do you want to stay?" Louder still. "Why do...you. stay? Why... want..." Her arms jerked violently as she talked and her body pushed back hard against her chair, head bobbing loosely against her chest. Silence. Everyone stayed as still and quiet, clinging to one another's hands.

From behind them, through the walls, the orchestra played the familiar strains of the Stabat Mater. Jody trembled. Only he knew.

Only he understood that the record player was unplugged and discarded carelessly on the floor behind the old painted door. He tried, desperately, but he was no longer empty, no longer open. He was so distracted by the music he hadn't even noticed Meg's body, seated right next to him, had gone limp.

Meg stood up, never breaking the clasping of their hands. Jody and Billy cried out in surprise. At first her lips stammered, and her body shook. Then she jolted, every muscle from foot through trunk still as a board. The voice that came from her lips was clear, but not her own. The strong voice of a little boy spoke plainly. "*Eia mater, fons amoris, me sentire vim doloris fac tecum lugeam.*"

The green light flashed on the Ghost-later, placed carefully between them. It dutifully translated in its feminine tone. "O Mother, fountain of love, make me feel the power of sorrow, that I may grieve with you."

A tear fell down Meg's dark cheek. "Fac me vere tecum flere."

"Let me sincerely weep with you," the computer voice tolled.

Ms. Austin stood up in a flash and threw off the hands of

those around her. Her face was contorted in a dark and twisted scowl. "*Fac me vere tecum flere. Fac me vere tecum flere,*" she mocked. Her voice sounded like a chorus of foreign vile shrieks all gathered into one throat, and her tone clearly mocking and full of disdain. "*You want to weep with me? Filthy urchin, I'd settle for you leaving me alone. Look what you've done!*"

"*Eia mater, fons amoris.*" The voice of the boy sounded sad and hurt as it leaked eerily though Meg's mouth.

The computer returned, "O Mother, fountain of love."

"*Shut your mouth. I don't love you. You're an animal.*"

The professor's neck craned. Her tendons that ran through it corded up and stretched long. She grunted and fought against the thing taking over her body, but could not overcome it.

Meg jumped up on the table and walked across on all fours like an angry dog coiled to strike. She turned her twisted snarling face this way and that, eye to eye with Ms. Austin. "*Quis est homo?*"

"Who is the human?"

Jody moved his mouth in a faint whisper, parroting what the computer said, desperately trying to make sense of it all. He watched as Ms. Austin struggled with everything she had against the beast inside her; muscles contorted and strained, teeth gnashed.

"*Who are you little girl? You think you can best me?*" The voice of the old woman ran up Jody's spine.

The ghost was angry with Ms. Austin, the woman whom she inhabited, who fought against her for control of her earthly husk. He had never felt an energy so vile and perverse. Her hand played with her own neck. Her fingers tracing the course of her jugular.

"*I can taste you little girl. Your blood smells delicious.*" The old hag's voice cracked and groaned as she fought for control of the professor's body.

"No!" Ms. Austin's voice broke through.

"*Can't I taste you, pretty please?*" The hag's voice mocked as it caused the professor's own fingers to scratch and claw at her neck.

"*Quis est homo?*" Meg growled in a low unearthly rumble.

"Who is the human?"

"No! Stop! Stop!" Ms. Austin pulled her hands away from her exposed jugular, leaving behind deep red claw marks.

"Enough!" Jody could take no more.

He leapt across the table and took her wrists in his own sweaty grasp, pulling down with all his might to assist her in the struggle against this strange evil.

The professor's body twisted, her head cocked sideways and looked down on Jody. "*Who are you?*"

"*Quis est homo?*" Meg growled again.

"Who is the human?"

Then both hag and boy let out hair raising laughter followed by screams. "Oh yes," they said in earie tandem. "He is the boy with the gun."

The old woman sauntered around the circle, using the Professor's body, and the boy, inside Meg, plopped around and sniffed and growled at Jody and Karen. The old woman stopped and patted Meg's body on the head. The tandem voice called out once more.

"The bearded one was here. We can smell him. Do it quick!"

The professor traced Jody's jaw line and pulled his chin up toward her face. "My dear boy, the dead see, and the dead speak."

"Ela mater, fons amoris."

"O Mother, fountain of love."

"Shut up child...mommy is speaking with the adults."

The boy whimpered through Meg's vocal cords and she sat, legs crossed on the table, politely waiting her turn.

"I've heard about you, Jody Howard. The dark man talks... a

lot. He followed you here. Do you remember him, Jody? He remembers you."

Jody strengthened his resolve and shoved Ms. Austin's cold, fleshy arm away from his face. "Shut up you old hag."

"Temper, temper," the old woman's voice clucked disapprovingly. "He talks to you too, doesn't he. He follows you home every night and whispers into your ear as you sleep. He remembers, and wants you to know... justice is coming."

The boy began giggling and squirming on the table in Meg's skin. The old woman walked back around to Ms. Austin's chair. She sat down, stoically, legs crossed under an unseen skirt. "Peter, it's almost time, don't you think?"

"Yay!" Meg clapped her hands and jumped down from the table and did an exquisitely child-like dance.

As she shuffled around the circle, she sang out, or rather, the boy sang through her. "Jody and Karen sitting in a tree. K-i-s-s-i-n-g. First comes love. Then comes marriage. Then comes Jody with the baby carriage."

A memory flooded through Karen's mind. It hadn't always been sad, but tonight she felt the odd and unsettling weight of shame down upon her shoulders. She felt the cold bathroom tile underneath her bare feet. She felt the pinch of the uncomfortably hard toilet seat under her thighs as she sat there in quiet, a few minutes too long for comfort. She lifted a thick white stick up to her eyes. The display was analog but bright and clear. A single pink line crossed unbroken across the aperture.

Karen snapped. "No! Stop!"

This wicked old woman wanted to take everything from her. The theft and ruination had already begun, the joy from her memory was gone. All that was left was a horrible empty feeling in her heart, in her womb, compelling her to hide. She couldn't let it steal more from her, from Jody. Her quivering body exploded from her seat. She pushed passed Ms. Austin, and ran through the store towards the door.

"Now you can go," the hag cackled.

Karen burst through the front door, the bell rattling nearly off of its mounts. Beyond the store came the sound of shrieking tires. Then, a chorus of gasps, every member of the Parapsychological Association having left the circle behind, huddled behind the great bay windows, peering out onto the street.

Ms. Austin fell to her knees where she was, sobbing uncontrollably, her voice her own once more. "I'm sorry, Jody. I'm so sorry."

Jody dashed through the store and onto the street. Just outside the door, a black car sat parked motionless in the dark street, its windshield shattered, fractured in oddly concentric circles. The driver walked toward the front of the vehicle audibly praying desperate vespers for mercy.

Jody ran to the front of the car and slid on his knees across the pavement. He reached out to touch her broken, motionless body, eyes fixated on the sky, hair still done in tight, careful curls. He lost himself in grief, pleading for her to live, only to be pulled to the curb by the arms of his best friend, Billy.

CHAPTER
TWENTY-FOUR

Jody lost track of the days since the dark pronunciation from the unknown, declaring him marked for death. Surely the angel of death, if such a thing even existed, had visited, but not as promised. It had come, and reaped a terrible harvest. Still, he breathed, slowly, in and out every morning as he lay in bed, alone. Death had come and once more cruelly passed him by.

Time no longer held meaning for him. Sometime after the first week, Meg had taken over operation of the store in his stead. It was about that time she began sending Billy to his house; to make sure he ate; to make sure he bathed.

It was all so exhausting; hearing him drone on; pretending he cared about what the latest headline was, or which celebrity did what to whom. He couldn't say how many times the sun had risen and fell behind his bedroom blinds, but he knew it had been months, not days.

He waited, seated at the edge of his bed, facing the dark empty bathroom. He had forgotten why he waited. Purpose was meaningless. His job meant nothing. He didn't want to work. He didn't want to put forth effort. So, he simply didn't.

Brown eyes pooled with bitter tears. He felt it coming, the

desperate emptiness that met him every time he tried to move, to rise from his lonely, empty bed.

The bottom of his feet began to tingle and burn. Toes, tapped uncomfortably on the crumb-laden carpet.

"It's there. Do it." The words slipped out more quiet than whispers. Goosebumps rose on his arms as a cold, stale draft swept over his skin. Palms itched. Hands shook.

"Do it."

He bent over. No need to look. He knew where it was. Timid fingers felt the metal; hard, smooth, cold. Carefully, he pulled the box out from under the bed frame. He laid it on his lap, as softly as a newborn babe, the weight of the squared edges biting into the skin of his knees. His thumb reached for the combination lock and hesitated.

The squeal of styrofoam clam shells scraping against one another intruded on the quiet solemnity of his bedroom. Something shuffled on Jody's tiny kitchen table.

"I got you a Broadcaster from the Mt. Adams Bar & Grill... huh... all that delicious hot goetta, got some Jalapeño Ravioli... doesn't get better than that, eh?" Billy tried his best to make his voice enticing, but it sounded more creepy than tempting.

The smell of hot food wafted down the hallway into Jody's bedroom. Part of him wanted to get up, shut the door, and finish it. Instead, he slipped the box back in place, put on a clean t-shirt and poked his head through the doorway.

"You don't need to bring me food." His voice shook.

He was hiding something and Billy could tell. Billy could always tell.

"Of course, I do, it's Tuesday, that's my day." His tone was questioning, and he peeked around the corner and down the hall toward his friend. "Meg will bring something tomorrow..."

"That's not what I mean." Jody slipped out of his shorts and into a pair of crumpled blue jeans hidden discretely behind his bedroom wall. "You don't have to keep bringing me food all the time."

"Meg says I have Tuesdays and Thursdays, that's good enough for me. So, until you start to return to the land of the living, I'll be bringing you food on Tuesdays and Thursdays."

Jody walked down the tiny hallway. He lifted up his hot, dripping sandwich and stared Billy down as he chewed.

"If I leave my apartment, will you leave me alone for one week, just one week?" He washed down the goetta and rye with a cold sip of soda.

Billy pondered his boss's proposition as he feasted on his own delicious takeout meal. Jody read the sly tilt of his eyebrows like a book. "I'm not going with you on the 4th of July to some stupid house party."

"Nah man, you've got me all wrong. I'll tell you what, if you'll go with me out to the Balloon Glow tonight, I'll blow some smoke Meg's way and she'll never know I didn't come here at all next week."

Jody hardly waited for his friend to finish his sentence. "Done."

Billy chuckled and spit as he tried to talk, laugh, and chew all at once. "Bro this is gonna' be off the chain."

Jody peered at Billy over his half-eaten sandwich with cowed and judgmental eyes. He had negotiated successfully for some peace and quiet at last.

His shattered nerves had grown slowly worse over the last few weeks. The relative peace and stability he felt with Karen had died with her, and his struggle to give up alcohol was so much harder this time than the last. It had almost drug him under, and he had convinced himself that somehow through all of this, his true peace could be found once more if Billy and Meg would just leave him alone. He finished his sandwich and stared blankly into the kitchen beyond Billy's chair, shoulders slumped, and sighed.

"Dude," Billy dropped his french-fry onto the table and pushed back his chair in disgust. "You saw it again didn't you?"

"No." Jody's voice cracked and his eyes watered with incredulity and the effects of the chunk of jalapeño he just crushed between his teeth. "I did not."

"Yes, you did. Don't lie to me, Jody. I know you did."

Jody relented. "I'm seeing her now. She's doing something in the kitchen...smiling. I think she's happy you're here." He buried his face in his hands, trying to rub the vision from his eyes and mind.

"You can't be seeing that crap man. No, I need you to get better."

"I can't help it if I see it. How am I supposed to stop seeing it?"

"I don't know man, just don't, okay." Billy picked up his wayward french-fry and shoved it into his mouth. "What did she look like this time?"

"In her pink dress, just like that day."

"Just the pink dress, not all crusty and nasty and dead?"

"Yes, just the pink dress."

Jody hated Billy's constant questioning. Remembering facts, formulas, basic information about the world was sometimes difficult for his friend. Jody couldn't understand how Billy couldn't remember those things but could remember every lurid detail of anything ever told him about the apparitions haunting his day-to-day life.

Billy made it his business, his job, to remember each and every haunt, every bout of depression, every time he got the shakes, and every time he fell victim to his PTSD. It should have endeared Billy to him, but somehow it only served to feed his resentment and longing for solitude.

The ghostly visions were becoming particularly prevalent of late. They were startling, and unpredictable. The apparitions came and went as they pleased. Jody had no control of how they manifested, sometimes as in death, sometimes as in life. There was never any way to know what he would see when things fluttered in from the waning focus of his peripheral vision. It was maddening in every sense.

"Well, at least it wasn't the dead one. I hate the dead ones." Billy spat out more tiny specks of partially chewed food as he spoke.

"How would you know which one you hate? You never see it." Jody slammed his soda can down on the table.

"I don't know man. I just hate hearing about it, okay."

"Well, I hate seeing it." Jody pushed his food back away from him. "It's killing me. I can't let her go if I see her all the time. I think... I think I'm going crazy."

"You've got to get out of this hole, Jody. You can't just mope around here all day. That, alone, is enough to drive you crazy." Billy began hurriedly gathering his leftovers and shoving them into the flimsy plastic bag with an unnaturally loud squeal of the foam clamshells. "Don't forget...tonight, at six."

TWENTY-FIVE

Rain fell in sheets and lightning flashed, strobing the bright yellow façade of a singular storefront nestled in a deep valley of the Red River Gorge in the hills of Eastern Kentucky. The façade looked more like a saloon from the pages of a novel about the old west, but the white sign hung at the curved apex of the roofline, the painted face of a wild-eyed hippie with flowing yellow hair, declared the establishment to be Miguel's Pizza, the regions only restaurant of note, and a favorite spot where Jody and his father would refresh themselves after long hot days of climbing. It was a landmark in a sea of green that could not be missed.

Jody stood, across the road, watching the rain beat and wind rattle the thin aluminum storm door, the Middle Fork of the Red River roaring behind him lapping at the bank, feet above its normal docile levels. Out of that flapping door stepped a man in a hooded black raincoat and blue jeans. His face shadowed from the thrashing lightning. He started walking, across the wet road, toward Jody.

~

"Watch what you're doing moron!" Billy's hands pulled, white knuckled, against the steering wheel. "Sorry guys." Traffic was heavy on the Combs Bridge. The line of cars stretched for miles down the highway, everyone jockeying for position, vying for the most advantageous route off I-275 down to historic Coney Island. The horn on the tiny car blared.

Jody's body was flung violently forward and then settled back hard against the pleather seat. It would have been worse had he not been jammed in between the bodies of his friends in a sweaty and uncomfortable press resulting from their feeble attempt to fit three people in a backseat designed for two.

"You were snoring so loud." Meg giggled. "What were you dreaming about? It must have been something good."

Jody ignored the question, and instead nodded politely. The way she smiled at him made him uncomfortable. It wasn't creepy. It just felt inappropriate. It didn't seem like enough time had passed since he lost her. Was there ever enough time? Could he ever truly heal from something like that?

Meg's eyes were a little too empathetic, shining, almost glistening with care and concern. He also wasn't fond of her touch. Her thigh and knee brushed against his. It couldn't be helped, there was no doubt, but it made his own skin crawl and his stomach turn. They were literally jammed cheek to jowl in that tiny car. He didn't blame her, but when her pinky gently grazed across his, he recoiled. Warmth of touch felt foreign and threatening.

His friends had showed compassion and cared for him through the aftermath of that awful night. Meg's sincerity was abundantly apparent, just like Billy's. He could forgive her for her role in the whole incident. Did she even need forgiving? She couldn't help what happened, at least he didn't think so, but what he couldn't forget, what he so far refused to forget, was Karen.

"Come on guys, let's go." Helen pulled on Billy's hand and drug the group through the maze of parked cars toward a swirling throng of people.

Jody spent his time mindlessly following Helen and Billy as they weaved from one outdated carnival attraction to another. Meg was a mere half step behind him, always ready to bring his attention to the amazing and beautiful things around them as soon as they entered her realm of perception. The bright lights were beautiful, blaring out against the sinking summer sunset. Mechanical rides buzzed and whirled, people laughed. It was lifting to her and she shared her awe at every turn.

"I wish I would have brought my swimsuit." Meg jabbed Jody in the ribs with her elbow bringing him out of his mindless trance.

Just on the other side of a steel link fence hundreds of people frolicked in the cool blue waters of Sunlight Pool. The massive oasis of blue water provided all comers relief from the smothering early July heat. It called to him. He pulled at the fence link and licked at dry cracking lips.

"That looks amazing."

Meg pulled at his belt loop with her bony finger. "Come on, it's closing soon anyway. Let's go." She pulled him in past the turnstiles and over to the concrete skirt at the edge of the giant pool. She sat down on an empty pool chair, removing her shoes and socks. "Come on, just dip your toes in," she giggled.

Laughter was intoxicating. It threatened him, threatened to take away some of the hurt he felt inside, and he didn't deserve to have that taken away, at least, he didn't think so. He wanted to forget, to leave behind his old choices, his mistakes, but he wasn't sure how.

That smile, it beamed in the sun, her cocoa skin sparkled, splashed with water. She wouldn't smile like that, not if she knew how he felt inside, not if she knew everything, not even if she just knew most things.

She didn't know about what was under the bed, how he thought about it all the time. Would she still look at him the same way? And smile?

"Come on, Jody. Please." She reached out her hand. She had soft hands, hands that wanted to help. He didn't want to scream, cry, or beg, but he needed help.

"I want to but..." Jody hesitated, focusing on the ground between his feet.

"Then do it," she urged.

Those words. He looked up. Those same words that followed him everywhere, now she was saying them. He winced. She wouldn't be saying them if she knew what they meant. Would she?

"Jody, come on. It's me. It's just me and some water. I wouldn't hurt you. Come on. Trust me. It feels great."

He nodded. "It's you."

He could barely say the words. He wanted to believe her, so badly. He wanted someone, something, anything to take those words and make them into something new, something different. So, he trusted.

Jody flipped off his shoes and tiptoed to the edge, gripping the curved tile lip with his toes. He had no more began to crouch toward the water when Meg came careening from her seat and leapt, dragging Jody with her, both fully clothed, into the deep.

The refreshing water welcomed him in and consumed his senses. It washed away the salts and heat from his sun burnt skin. He felt weightless in the depths and kicked easily toward the surface even while clad in waterlogged clothes. His head burst through the surface and he gasped in a chest full of fresh evening air. Meg splashed and howled beside him.

"See! Beautiful!"

170

He had to agree. "Oh my gosh, this is great!" He felt invigorated, charged, refreshed.

Eventually, they both pulled themselves up out of the water and sat dripping on the edge, dangling their legs over the side. He smiled, and they talked. He had a conversation with Meg, nothing serious, just pleasant conversation. He couldn't remember the last time he was able to just talk and enjoy someone else's presence.

"Dude! There you are!" Billy called to him from behind the fence. "Come on it's almost time man!"

They followed him deeper into the throng, through aging carnival rides, food stands, games. Jody beheld a sight that caused him to gasp from its striking visual beauty.

Giant glowing orbs slowly rose up from the darkening earth into the growing twilight, clad in bold geometric patterns of striking colors. Some found release from their bonds and lifted up into the freedom of the heavens, and others stayed tied to terra firma with great thick strands of rope. They walked slowly amongst the glowing orbs. The wicker gondola baskets felt massive and enchanting in an oddly visceral way.

He was small. He was less, and so were all the troubles he left behind him on the other side of the busy Combs bridge.

Meg wrapped her hand around his bicep and pulled in close. "I'm glad you came out with us tonight, thank you. Things really are a lot more fun with you around."

Jody smiled an awkward, half-hearted smile. "It's only been..."

"I know." Meg drew her foot through the loose dirt and gravel beneath them. "You're important to us, Jody, all of us."

He didn't know what to do with that sentiment and the reassuring pressure from Meg's grip, but he chose to accept it, on faith that it was deserved.

Jody stepped up to a carnival game, politely separating himself from Meg's grasp. He pointed wryly toward a large stuffed penguin pinned to the prize board. Meg smiled in antic-ipation and nodded her approval.

"Great shot!" Meg bounced and cheered him as he deftly downed a tiny target in the center of a moving metal duck with an overpowered squirt gun.

Jody didn't smile back. He froze. Amongst the din of laughing families and dinging carnival bells a peculiar laugh echoed from somewhere just behind his head.

"Did you hear that?"

"What?" Meg was concerned. He had snapped. One of those visions were taking over his shattered mind again.

"A kid."

"There's lots of kids." Meg drew closer, begging him not to make a scene, gently pulling at his shirt.

"No, it sounded like a kid was laughing and just ran right by me."

"I didn't see anything."

Jody swallowed hard. "Me either."

As he scanned the crowd, he caught a glimpse of a child darting between a couple of the gondola baskets. He drug Meg in the direction of the fleeting vision.

"There!" He saw it again, darting the other way further down the row. Together, they ran, trying desperately to catch up.

"What is that?" Meg panted, breathlessly.

"You heard it too? Just now?"

Meg shook her head, yes.

They waited, quiet and still amongst the swirling press of people. Behind Jody, boisterous children cackled and screamed, playing all manner of games of chance.

An unexpected pop exploded through the air. It was sharp, jarring, and louder by far than anything else near him.

It happened again. Jody jerked involuntarily. Again, the loud crack echoed and Jody fell to his knees. "No, no, no" he muttered and fell onto the dusty beaten path.

"Jody!" Meg rushed to his side in time to see his eyes roll back in his head and him stammer something unintelligible as he continued to shake violently.

He lay there convulsing, trying to fight for clarity, anxiety and fear coursing through his veins and foggy mind on the speedy wings of an uncontrolled adrenaline rush. His hearing was gone, the whole world around him silent as the grave, but through vibrating, jarring eyes he could still see, make out smatterings of discernible images, and as a crowd gathered around him, he pieced together one final picture through a shuffling mass of legs and feet.

Just beyond the gathering crowd, a child peeked out from behind a gondola basket and laughed at him, with a cheshire grin under an old-time scally cap.

TWENTY-SIX

J ody's universe crumbled into smoldering embers around his feet. PTSD reared its ugly head again, rising from the depths of his depression.

He rode, silently in the night, every bump of Billy's car forcing his forehead harder against the cool foggy glass of the rear passenger window. He was too embarrassed to speak, wanting not even to breathe. The only thing he desired was sleep, but even the fitful slumber of his regular course of nightmares shut their doors to him.

Meg sat even closer to him than she had on the way to the festival. Her arm was tucked gently and politely around the small of his back, hand grasping at his hip. He could feel the weight of her cheek against his shoulder and could feel her delicate, caring eyes fixed on his sweat muddled complexion.

"Balloons, and darts? How could the sound of popping balloons do this?"

Billy scrunched his mouth tight and squeezed the wheel hard in his grasp. "No reason, I guess. It just did."

"I can't believe after all these years..." dear, sweet Helen, was interrupted with an unnatural cough coming from her boyfriend in the driver's seat.

"Just…don't. Us all talking about it like this is not going to help."

Jody watched the cityscape scroll by as they squabbled over the bones of his life. The car turned onto a street Jody knew well. He counted every building until he came to the one he had poured his heart and soul into. The windows were black, the once happy façade now dull and lifeless.

He looked for the tiny white sign emblazoned with the word "Closed" he had placed on the door months ago. Instead, in the doorway he saw the dark silhouette of a man standing facing the old wooden door.

"Stop!"

"Oh my God! Jody you scared me to death!"

"Stop the car Billy! Stop! Stop!"

The wheels of the car squealed and the car careened into a sideways stop on the otherwise abandoned city street. His fellow passengers groaned and voiced their disapproval. Jody pulled hard on the plastic handle and nearly fell out of the car onto the pavement. The dark silhouette turned to face the commotion and Jody marched to meet it.

The dark figure spoke. "Jody?" His long beard and steely eyes sparkled in the light of the streetlamp.

"D-Donald?" Jody took a step back. "What are you doing here?"

"I was just out for a walk and thought I'd stop by for a cup of coffee."

There was no corner of the universe in which Don's story could be believed. Jody simply glossed over it. "We're closed."

"I can see that."

Jody had no reply. Finally, he just blurted out, "Good."

"Good?" The bearded man waived his arm toward the door. "How can this be good?"

Billy threw the car into park and yelled out the window. "Jody! Get in the car!"

Meg came running up behind him. "Jody? Is there something I can help you with?"

Donald huffed. "I think you all have done quite enough."

Jody could feel the tug of Meg's tiny hands against the back of his shirt. He politely motioned for her to stop. "Don, just tell me the truth. Why are you here?"

Donald halted. The words stuck in his throat not wanting to be released into the world and subject themselves to the critical eyes of others. "I'm here... because I'm supposed to be here."

"Why would you want to be here?" Meg asked.

"Who said anything about wanting to be here?" He turned and paced nervously, mindlessly rubbing at his freshly shaven head.

"No one." Jody replied.

"Exactly!" the elderly man shook a quick index finger in Jody's face and then turned to pace once more. He stroked his chest length beard, as if to garner strength from its wiry strands. "I was sent here."

"Who sent you here?" Jody snapped back. "The boy?"

"What?" Donald seemed genuinely surprised. "No... the... why would the..."

"Who?"

Donald grimaced and rolled his eyes. "Please don't make..."

"Who sent you, Don?"

The old man stroked his beard and swiveled his head to and fro as if fighting some unseen bridle. "I am." Donald blurted.

"You?... Sent yourself?"

"No 'I AM' sent me... the I AM." He turned away mumbled to something unseen in a tone never intended for Jody and Meg to hear. "There! I said it, are you happy?"

Meg tugged at Jody's arm. "Okay, Mr. Donald has gone off the deep end with unicorns and the Easter Bunny, let's get out of here."

"I'm not crazy." Donald insisted, pacing again. "I'm just not used to this kind of thing."

Billy called from far behind them. "Lets go! This is a street not a parking lot!"

"I am the mouthpiece of Jahova, the most powerful being in the universe." Donald's voice strained as he tried to cover up his reluctant delivery.

"This man is crazy." Meg looked at Donald, flabbergasted, then looked confused at Jody. "Do you not think this man is crazy? Why are we still standing here?"

Donald tried to compose himself. "I am of the Unseen, a servant of God."

Meg turned and tried to walk away. Jody stopped Meg from leaving, with a gentle touch of his hand against her.

"Okay, Don, let's assume I believe you. You are a mouthpiece. What are you supposed to tell me?"

The strange man cleared his throat, and breathed in deeply, steeling his countenance. The words still sounded unsure, though his face was resolute. "Fear not. The truth will set you free."

"Alrighty then!" Meg pulled Jody away from the crazy old man, forcing him to stumble after her down the sidewalk and out into the street.

He fought free from her grip.

"What are you talking about?"

Jody was confused, indignant. This strange man had come from nowhere, insulted the way he had shut down after everything that had happened, and had the gall to spew some kind of encouraging word, wrapped in a vague platitude.

Don's face was filled with consternation. His eyes welled, cheeks red, lips quivering. "I don't know. That's all I have."

CHAPTER
TWENTY-SEVEN

Jody tossed and turned in the night. Sweat beaded on his brow and his feet roiled, knotting themselves in sheet and cover. He groaned and rumbled, mumbling incoherently into the darkness.

A light flashed and his body ceased movement. In the stillness he breathed deeply, relieved that he was no longer there, he was no longer trapped in the truck with the body of his headless father.

His fists tensed and the muscles in his forearm bulged in their straining. The world around him began materializing from white, into the fabric of reality. It was happening again, cycling from one horrible scene to another. His heart pounded and he breathlessly whispered "no" before falling motionlessly into his next dream.

The kitchen of his mother's rental cabin was dark. Gathering clouds outside had just turned the brightness of midday into dusk. He could taste the malty sweetness of whisky on his breath. He fiddled a single key on a flat tear shaped fob labeled "#1 Son," and a brand new molded black mortarboard emblazoned with a yellow "2015."

Billy knocked on the table with his fist, demanding his

attention. "Hey, did you hear what I just said? He wants to talk to you. We've been looking for this guy for years and we finally found him."

"How can you be sure he was the one?"

"He told me himself. He remembers the whole thing, blacking out and hearing a horn. He saw the crash in his rearview mirror after he got control of the car. He told me the exact date, man, no prompting on my part."

"...and he was drunk?"

"You know he was... spent the night partying down in the rock shelter."

"What would he have to say to me?"

"I don't know...Sorry...I guess." Billy pulled the keys from Jody's grasp. "Listen, we've got two days until we have to leave for college. You do this now and get some closure or you may never have the opportunity again."

Jody gripped his keys tight. He pushed his seat back with a shove and started to get up when Billy reached across the table and grabbed his hand.

"I'll drive you."

The world cut to white. Jody could feel the covers restricting his movement. He kicked at them and moaned like a child throwing a great fit. He tried, but he couldn't wake. His heart sped up again. It was coming. He couldn't stop it. He screamed, but all that materialized in the physical realm was a pitiful whimper.

That voice, that deep, horrible voice, spoke clearly in his head. "I want you. Do it. Do it!"

Thunder rolled and he was standing in the rain, across the street from Miguel's. The dark man stood in the doorway. He stepped, slowly, out into the maelstrom. Jody lifted the square glass bottle to his lips and turned it up, sucking down the last few drops and flinging it hard against the pavement.

"There, see, he wants to talk." Billy pointed toward the man through the beating rain.

Jody, stepped out onto the blacktop, crunching underfoot shards of broken glass and the tattered remnants of a black label.

He didn't want to see this, not now, not for the hundredth time. He sat up and broke through the dream into the waking world.

"I don't want to!" he screamed.

His eyes opened, wide, taking in the room around him. He felt it. The pull to the thing beneath the bed. He wanted it. He needed it, the relief that it promised, the end, the blackness, the peace.

"Do it." The voice growled again in his mind.

Meg jumped in reaction to Jody's scream. She had been leaning against the doorjamb, watching him try to sleep.

"You never get any rest, do you?"

Jody panted and pawed at the covers, untangling his legs and pulling the sheet back over his stomach. "No, not really."

Billy stuck his head through the door. "Everything okay?"

"What were you dreaming about anyway?" Meg asked, arms folded.

Jody looked at Billy, ignoring Meg's question.

"Well..." Meg persisted.

"Come on, let's leave him alone." Billy tried to usher her back into the tiny hallway.

Meg pushed him away. "Jody?"

"Wait," Jody spoke up as he pulled the covers off completely and stood up beside the bed. "Billy, I need you to do something for me."

He kneeled and pulled a black metal box from underneath the bed. Tired fingers worked the tumblers on a simple combination lock. A latch released and the spring-loaded door popped open in a flash. From the box he pulled out an object.

He admired it in his hand. It was weighty but molded to fit in his hand and perfectly balanced.

"Where did you get a gun?" Meg gasped.

"I've had it for a long time." He pulled back the slide and confirmed that that chamber was empty. Mouth tightly clinched, hand shaking, he handed the weapon to his best friend.

Billy received it and weighed it carefully in his hands. "What do you want me to do with it?"

"Take it home. Put it away in a safe place. I'll take it back when I'm ready...I thought I was ready, but I'm not."

"I told you. You should have thrown it in the river a long time ago."

"But I didn't." Jody's tone was insistent and clear. "And you won't either. Keep it safe."

Billy brushed past Meg and walked straight out the front door. He offered no explanations or apologies, and never even offered her a passing glance.

"Jody," Meg asked meekly. "What are you doing?"

"Trying to sleep."

CHAPTER
TWENTY-EIGHT

The cold, dark movie theater held only loneliness. Jody felt it wash over him, cocoon him, even amongst dozens of silhouettes seated beside him.

The plush heated seats reclined in order to offer the perfect viewing experience. It felt frivolous, awkward. He didn't want to be watching a movie, especially in a dark, crowded theater.

Deep inside, he contracted back into his shell of self-loathing. Mindlessly, he crunched on popcorn as ads flew by on the giant silver screen. Meg's hand grazed his own as they tussled each for their own share of the buttery popped kernels, temporarily interrupting his self-imposed isolation.

"Tasty. This is delicious, isn't it?" She chewed and smiled at him through the waxing and waning colors of the movie projector. She was growing on him.

She was an ever-present force in his world now, just like Billy, but different. She watched, she helped, she listened, but not because she was always there, it was because, he thought, she wanted to be there, with him, in the night. She was not bound to him in any way, but always wanted to be there.

He slurped at his tart, large cherry slushy and he felt his phone rumbling in his pocket. "Ugh, I forgot to..." He pulled the phone out and the screen blared at him "Professor". "I'll be right back. He darted to the exit and pushed through the heavy double swinging doors out into the noisy hallway.

"Hello?" The voice on the other end of the line was garbled with a hiss of background noise and digital distortion. "Hello, Dana? Professor?"

"Jody... Jody... can you hear me?"

"Yes."

"I can see him."

"What are you talking about?"

"I'm sitting... in my living room... and I see a dark man standing in the corner."

A chill flew up Jody's spine. "I told you we're done. I'm not interested in..."

"He won't stop talking to me. I had to call. He won't shut up."

"What are you talking about?"

"The dark man wants me to tell you that he wants to talk to you." Her voice dimmed but Jody could still hear her. "See, here, I called him. Here, you can talk to him."

The phone squealed. Static stabbed at Jody's eardrum. He exclaimed and dropped his phone on the well-trodden carpeted floor. He didn't even try to listen to it again. When he bent over to pick it up, he pressed the red phone icon.

He shoved it back into his pocket and walked back into the cavernous theater, now well populated with fellow movie goers. Jody kicked up his footrest and was twenty seconds into his first preview approved for general audiences when he noticed Meg was staring at him, only him, not saying a word and not eating anything.

"What?" he asked with some disdain. Meg pointed over his shoulder to the gentleman seated to his other side. Once he saw her finger, he could feel it in his bones, so he wasn't shocked when he turned and faced the bald and bearded man in the impeccable suit.

"Fancy seeing you again," Donald said in hushed tones.

"Yes... fancy." Jody snarked.

"Can we step outside?"

"Oh, I think we should."

The hallway was now empty. Loud rumbles and crescendos leaked into the corridor weaving a contorted tapestry of discord in the air around them.

"I'm the last person you want to see right now..."

"You think?"

"Have you thought about what I told you the other night?"

"Not really."

That was a lie. Donald's brief and simple message had sat with him, moved into his subconsciousness, and frustratingly stared him down with no end. He couldn't wrap his mind around it, learn from it and fashion it into something that could be of good use.

"Ghosts are lies." Donald shuffled away and leaned on the opposite wall. "They are not what they purport to be."

Jody stared, not uninterested, but not wanting to be there, listening to this mad man preach to him from his pulpit of experience.

"They are a poison and seek to eat away at your soul."

"Goodnight, Don." Jody turned away intending to leave his benefactor behind in the dust just as he had left Professor Austin after that horrible night.

Donald turned his back and frantically paced, hands on his bald head. "I told you he wouldn't want to listen to..." He stopped mid-sentence and raised his voice. "You are being poisoned, Jody!"

Jody stopped but did not turn to see the suited man behind him. "I know."

"But you don't have to be. I told you before, this is not your fault. Leave that thing alone. You didn't listen, and now you are paying the price. Karen... the baby... it's trying to kill you." He pulled nervously at his beard and tried to maintain at least some composure. "And it's my fault."

Jody turned. Donald leaned in, hands on his knees as if speaking those words were vile, like vomiting on a sidewalk. He walked up to the bearded man. "Karen... is... dead. My child... is... dead. What did you do?"

"Nothing, Jody. Nothing." Donald's voice cracked and his lip quivered. "I'm so sorry."

Jody lifted a balled fist to Donald's bowed head. It shook there for a moment, in anger. Then, one by one he forced his fingers to open, and he lay a trembling hand on the old man's shoulder. "I... just want to understand." Jody stepped once more toward the theater door.

"I know, but you don't need to, not yet." Donald righted himself and straightened his jacket. "You just have to be willing to try."

Jody became indignant. "Try? Haven't I done enough? I've lost...everything. I'm working on myself, but I can't even...". Jody paced, unable to hold his body still. "...I can't even stay by myself in my own apartment. I'm broken. I am trying all that I can try."

"I know." Donald said softly. "I'm sorry. You're starting exactly where you need to start."

"I can't get it out of my mind. No matter what I do. I close my eyes and it's all still there, the pain, the..."

"Forgiving is easy, Jody. Forgetting is harder." He opened his suit coat and placed his weathered hands on his hips. "Forgiving yourself is the hardest work of all."

A single tear trickled down Jody's cheek. "What do you know about forgiveness?" He asked breathlessly.

"Not as much as I should."

Jody sniffled and wiped his reddening eyes dry. "So, you're a prophet of God. What have you come to tell me this time?"

Donald chuckled softly and shook his head. "I don't know what I am, Jody. But you should know something much bigger than you or I is at work here. You are fighting for your life, every day, but I'm here to tell you, the fight is for your very soul."

He turned around quickly and fussed through clinched teeth. "I can't do that...he'll think I'm stupid."

"What?... What is it?"

"That's not all, Jody. There's something else I have to do."

Jody looked at him blankly for what seemed like hours.

The elder bald and bearded man finally rolled his eyes and talked to something invisible over his shoulder in hushed tones. "If I do that here and now, I will be the laughingstock of the entire... Why? Just tell me that. Why?"

When he was sufficed that he had lost his attempted argument with the invisible being, he gave a harumph and straightened his jacket. "I am required to do something, Jody... and I do definitely apologize, but may I look into your eyes?"

Jody leaned in. He looked at the old man's eyes intently. They bulged and stared at him like sparkling blue daggers. Those eyes alone were enough to unnerve even the most jaded of dispositions, but suddenly this strange old man in a well pressed suit leapt upon him.

"Not close enough!" he exclaimed as he grasped Jody's face.

His index fingers and thumbs pressed hard into the malleable skin that lay on Jody's cheeks and forehead. They pulled wide his eyelids and set his eyeballs to nearly bursting in their sockets. The old man, so close now their pupils nearly touched, hummed like a gardener quietly plying his craft. The song was sweet and eerie, and it only lasted but a moment when just as suddenly, he stopped dead silent and gasped.

"No! No, no, no!"

He pushed Jody away with his calloused and powerful

hands. The young man tripped backwards and fell into a padded bench along the walls of the corridor.

"Why would you show me that?" The bald man grimaced in disgust. All the blood drained from his face. He was pale, scared, and in that moment, looked as if he'd been beset by a million horrible thoughts that his aged flesh could not contain. He ran for the door, pushing through patrons and workers alike.

The red Slurpee straw hung on Meg's lip, her eyes propped wide in a dumbfounded stare. She had seen the whole thing from her silent perch just inside the screening room entrance.

"That man is coo coo for Coco Puffs." The straw fell from her lip. "Jody, are you okay?"

They walked out into the night, never finishing their movie. Jody was too embarrassed. He didn't want to spend one more minute in that place; people were everywhere, staring at him. He could feel their judgmental eyes. It caused the hair on the back of his neck to rise up and graze his collar every time he moved.

They both sat in Jody's car and closed the doors with a thud. All small talk stopped, the embarrassed feelings stopped. It was silent, still, and calm. Jody sighed in relief and Meg slurped the last of her slushy.

"Well, that wasn't so..."

Tap, tap, tap.

Hard, white knuckles rapped on Jody's window. On the other side of the glass, backlit by the flickering blue-green streetlights stooped Donald, stern-faced and staring back at him.

"Don't do it." Meg pleaded. "Jody, don't you... uh uh, I know you're not... Jody!"

The window rolled down very slowly as Jody cranked the antiquated manual handle almost against his will and definitely against his better judgment.

"What do you want, Don?"

"He's a crazy man, Jody! Start up the car and get out of here."

The old man winced and scrunched his brow. "I know I look crazy, but I'm not. I promise you."

Jody gave in to Meg's insistence and started the car. He was about to throw the car into gear when Don reached his hand in through the window and grabbed the steering wheel.

"I am NOT crazy!"

"Get off me!" Jody tugged at the old man's arm in an unsuccessful attempt to free the car.

"You can't sleep..." Don struggled to keep his hand around the steering wheel. "Not because you aren't able to...because you don't want to."

Jody stopped struggling.

"You don't want to see it again... any of it, the wreck, your dad, the dark man... you'd rather forget about it and never remember it all ever again... but you have to, Jody. You have to remember, or all the dead, decaying things from your past will pull you right down into the grave with them."

The car engine shuttered to a stop.

"No! Jody, don't, please!" Meg pleaded again.

He let go of Don's forearm and grabbed at Meg's hand, giving her a reassuring squeeze.

"How did you know about that... any of that?"

"I saw it in your eyes, the dream you have every night."

"And day... any time I fall asleep, it eventually happens if I sleep long enough. You saw that? In my eyes?"

The old man smiled through his shadowy beard. "Yes. I saw that and so much more. I saw your visions of Karen. I saw it all."

Meg's large slushy cup fell to the floorboard with a thud. "What in the..."

"Get in the car, Don."

CHAPTER
TWENTY-NINE

"Do you have any idea how hard it is to be transformed from upright, stalwart businessman to blithering idiot at a moment's notice? It is quite disconcerting."

The strange bearded man rattled on in the back seat as the car rumbled through the city on its quest. "I'd rather be... be..." his voice trailed off and he lowered his head. "No, I suppose I wouldn't want that."

"Do you have any idea what he's going on about?" Meg hissed.

Jody replied with a briefly shaken head and a cross look.

"How am I supposed to sit here and listen to this buffoon, Jody?"

"Faith! You are my savior and my prison." The old man yelled again from the rear, as he was wont to do on this short but agonizing trip, causing everyone in the front of the car to jump uncontrollably out of their seats.

"Listen, Don, could you just not yell right into my ear." Jody grumbled, waiting to turn left at yet another red light.

"Sorry, Jody." He folded his hands neatly in his lap and managed for an entire block to say nothing, to do nothing, but look out his window at the passing buildings in flickering city lights.

"Jody," he spoke up politely, waiting several breaths on his driver's acknowledgement. "You know, the truth will set you free."

The car squealed to a halt and Jody turned all the way around in his seat. "Okay, now listen here. I've had just about enough of your nonsense. If you don't...".

Without so much as uttering another syllable or even looking at another soul in the vehicle, Donald unlatched his seatbelt and calmly got out of the car.

"Here we are," he mouthed quietly, as Jody got out and unleashed a gusty tirade on the old man's bones. But he was unfazed, looking, through sparkling golden eyes, steadfastly at the old familiar storefront he had once called home. "Where it all began."

Jody stopped screaming, yelling at someone totally oblivious to his existence had not brought the cathartic relief he had hoped. He stepped around Don, ogling him like some novel museum display, all the while Don never lost focus. He snapped his fingers three times in the old man's face, nothing, not even a flinch.

"When things are broken beyond repair, sometimes it is best to go back to the beginning." The old man's eyes still never left the storefront across the abandoned street, and his voice barely raised above a whisper.

"Pick up the pieces, the big old nasty ones that are gnarled and hard to put your hands around. Those old pieces are what you have to pick up first, clear them out, before anything new can be built in their stead."

Jody was exasperated. "What are you talking about? I don't understand."

"Inside that old brick building, Jody, are monsters of our own design. We didn't make the monsters, per se, but we lived with them, fed them, gave them all the power and information they ever needed to suck every drop of life out of our souls. They must be dealt with." He bent low and looked Jody in the eye again. "But before we can even step foot back into that place, we have to clean ourselves out of the lies they use to manipulate us."

"And you did that... you cleaned yourself out of all the nasty stuff inside so you could be God's mouthpiece or whatever?" Jody's blood boiled. He was so filled with confusion, hate, fear. He couldn't see, he didn't want to see a way out.

"I don't want to be like you, old man. I don't want to be God's puppet. You're crazy. I'm... I'm not..." He had to fight back tears just to even say the words. "I'm not crazy."

"Nope, you're not wrong there, Jody." the old man popped upright. "You are most definitely not crazy, but God doesn't want you to be me."

"Then what does he want from me?"

The old man sat on a low stone retainer wall by the sidewalk. He nestled into the most comfortable position possible and picked up an unremarkable pebble. He rolled it over and over again in his fingertips and finally threw it down the street with a flick of his wrist.

"Pick up the rocks."

Meg burst out of the car and put her hands on Jody's shoulders, holding him close, carefully positioning herself between him and the insane and sharply dressed man behind them.

"Jody, come on, let's go. You don't have stay here and listen to that stupid old man anymore."

"I'm okay."

She wiped a tear away as it slid down his cheek. "You aren't okay, Jody."

"She's right, you're not, you know." The old man bellowed from his perch. "You're being eaten up, from the inside out, by guilt. You can't take it anymore. You can't run anymore. You can't hide. The truth will set you free."

"You're no preacher." Jody croaked, trying to right himself.

"You're right. I only have one word to give, no eloquent three-point homilies, no spectacular exercises in exegesis. I have been given one sentence for you, Jody Howard. The truth will set you free. That's all I got."

The old man stood up, dusted off the seat of his pants, and slowly started walking away, down the sidewalk.

"What does that even mean?" Jody called after Don, his voice cracking.

"She cares about you, Jody. She'll listen. Tell her the truth... about the dark man."

CHAPTER
THIRTY

Rain fell over Jody's body and beat him like a thousand tiny pebbles. He was soaked to the bone. All of his clothes clung to him in a strange and heavy way he had never quite experienced before. He found it hard to move, and hard to breathe. He was bound in chains of water, pressing him into the earth from whence he came.

"See, he wants to talk to you!" Billy's voice strained, trying to speak over the roar of water falling all around them.

Across the two lane road, the shadowy figure of a man stood in the doorway of Miguel's Pizza. He stepped forward into the storm. The black, hooded poncho gave him an ominous bat-like appearance through the mist and pouring rain. Step, by step, he floated out into the middle of the gravel parking lot and stopped, staring at the two of them.

Jody's fist clinched tight. His nails dug into his palm until red tinges of blood flowed down from his hands with the streams of rainwater. "I hate him, Billy. I don't even know him, and I hate him with everything in me."

"It's now or never, Jody! Go talk to him!"

He gulped down the last swig from his fifth of Jack Daniel's. It burnt his tongue and warmed his throat. It no longer gave him courage. He had drunk so much these last two years that a few drinks had very little effect, though the routine of sipping from the cold glass bottle gave him comfort. He smashed the bottle against the pavement and walked out across the street.

The dark man's face was still concealed in shadow under a hood, though his eyes twinkled out a faint blue shimmer from the dancing stormy skies. Jody wanted to see him, face to face. The physical inability to look upon him, to take in all of his features, added insult to injury. The fury inside him grew.

"Who are you?" Jody screamed out over the storm.

"It doesn't matter."

"I am Jody Howard." He beat his chest with great splashing thuds. The blows jarred his heart but did nothing to dissuade the focus of those black things he clung to and hid deep inside his chest. "You killed my father!"

"I know." He hung his head low, bowing to the pressure of the torrents and gales that lapped at his flesh like dogs at a steak.

"You almost killed me!"

"Yes." He shook his head and with an open palm covered his steely blue eyes. He shook. He wept, his sorrow unheard over the pelting rain.

Jody did not see the hidden tears. It wouldn't have mattered if he had. His rage boiled over as he lashed out at the dark man, hiding behind shame and rain.

"I hate you!" He screamed behind a shaking fist.

The man looked up. "I do too."

He pulled off his hood. Through the veil of the storm, he bore all, his hair, his eyes, his complete and utter sorrow.

Jody remained unmoved. "You're a monster! You ruined my life!"

He unleashed a hail of epitaphs and curses, trying with all his might to take his pound of flesh by wounding the dark

194

man's spirit. His words did not slake his lust for blood, but they tore down the dark man.

The man moaned from deep in his stomach. "I can't sleep. I close my eyes and I see it over and over again. I dream about it every night. I'm dying inside!"

The man had been thrown into such a strong, emotion driven frenzy that he convulsed and vomited onto the rain soaked gravel. He wiped the sick away from his mouth with a wet forearm. "I can't change what I did, Jody. I can't change anything."

"I can." Jody reached for the small of his back. He thrust his hand behind his sloppy waterlogged shirt and pulled out a grey handgun with his bloody hand. It was heavy. The carved wooden scales on the handle bit deep and firm into the fresh wounds on his palm.

It was his father's gun. He had taken it from the safe under his mother's bed weeks ago. He wasn't quite sure what for. It made him feel closer to his dad somehow.

His father loved to shoot. He went to the range all the time. His passion for guns was an affinity he had passed along to his son over countless weekends and shared moments together. It sat quietly in his top drawer of his bedroom dresser, and then was buried deep under his night clothes and underwear in his suitcase when they left on their last vacation before the big move to Cincinnati for college.

When Billy came back to the cabin after a late-night party with the locals, he told Jody all about the man he found drinking alone, drowning his sorrows in as much booze as he could throw down his throat.

It was then, as he nursed his fourth Budweiser in the dark kitchen, his mother and everyone else blissfully sleeping in their rustic beds, unaware, he decided what he would do. He decided every word, every action, every single step he planned carefully from beginning to end.

Now, it was done, every word spoken, every step taken, every act performed save the very last. All that remained was to pull the trigger.

The dark man stood, motionless, breathing deeply, eyes red, face bare, staring down the barrel of Jody's justice. His lips quivered. He offered no resistance, no fear, all apologies ceased. "Well... Do it!" His words shook Jody to his core. "Do it!" Jody steeled himself and steadied his shaking hand.

"Jody! Nooooo!" Billy leapt between them and struggled with Jody, stripping the firearm from his grasp. It landed in the mud and gravel, just out of reach. "Jody! Stop! Don't do it man! No!"

They fought, rolling in the sopping wet filth, gravel gnawing through clothing and flesh. Jody was consumed. He fought free and threw himself toward the weapon, but before his hand touched metal, the dark man bent down and picked it up. Jody and Billy stopped cold, all eyes fixated on the armed stranger looming over them. He turned it over in his hand, fumbling, trying not to lose his grip.

The man's face contorted into pure sorrow. His drooping frown pulled streams of tears from his eyes and his breath puttered as he spoke.

"I didn't mean it." His voice strained as he cried. "I promise. I didn't mean it." He raised the wet gun to his temple, and he pulled the trigger.

The exit wound was gaping and clear, but it did not mire his face. It was as if the whole side of his head exploded into the torrent. His body fell to the earth and lay, propped up on its side. The dark man's perfect and unspoiled face stared back at Jody, the hovering, gaping wound draining into the gravel, those perfect steel blue eyes never flinching, never closing, begging to be heard.

～

Meg became suddenly aware of her hand covering her gaping mouth and took it down. "I had no idea, Jody."

Instinctively, she put her arms around his neck and cradled his head in her hand. He surrendered to her sincerity and care. He put his head on her shoulders and cried, wetting her blouse with his tears.

It felt good and right to tell the story, all of it. Although he wept, the sorrow felt good as it left his body, like steam through the neck of a boiling kettle.

"Look at me, Jody. Look at me."

She put her hands on each side of his face and stared intensely. "It's not your fault. Do you hear me. You don't have to blame yourself for any of that, okay, not your dad, not that man, none of it. It's not on you."

Jody shook his head in agreement, but he cried even more. She was right, as always. He knew it wasn't his fault and now he could breathe and let that poison go that had been bottled up inside for so long.

"The truth, Jody! It sets you free!" Donald's voice danced to them on the evening urban breeze. His laugh bounced from one side of the street to the other.

"I thought he left." Meg whispered nervously.

Donald was the proverbial fly on the wall, ever present and never perceived. It was an off-putting quality which Jody did not appreciate.

"Go away!"

Donald did not leave. He put his hands in his pinstriped and perfectly pressed pockets and walked, slowly, towards them. His patent leather wingtips clicked on the sidewalk, marking perfect measure. His face was held low, eyes looking only at the ground, but glowed a steely blue in the florescent wash of the street lamps.

The footfalls ceased, mere feet from them. He never looked

up, lips fixed in a half-hearted smile. "Meg, my dear, I think it's time you should go."

She pulled Jody closer. "I don't know what you are, Don, but you can't have him."

The old man, chuckled softly, still transfixed on the sidewalk before his feet. "I don't *want* him. I have *wanted* nothing but the best for him for years, since before he can remember. I am not to be feared, Meg, but I am not to be trifled with. Leave us. It's up to Jody whether he sees the morning, but if you stay, I cannot guarantee the same for you."

She relented, letting Jody's arms slip from her grasp and backing all the way to Billy's car. She watched them both, carefully, not knowing if she had made the right choice, not knowing if this crazy old man was telling the truth. Donald may have been crazy, but she knew one thing he was not, was a liar.

Billy's car peeled off down the road, leaving Jody and his benefactor alone on that lonely sidewalk across the street from the old shuttered storefront full of his self-doubt and deferred dreams.

"I need you to remember, Jody," the old man's voice trailed off on the soft evening breeze, "Father's Day weekend in the Red River Gorge."

THIRTY-ONE

Donald leveled his gaze, raising his eyes from the sidewalk to meet Jody's stare. His cold grey eyes sparkled with flecks of gold, like sunshine itself.

"Look at me! Right here." The old man pointed at his eyes.

Jody gasped. Knees weakened and failed, causing him to fall backward. He tried to crawl away. "No, no, it can't be. Meg! Meg!"

"Stay with me. Stay right here." The old man knelt down still motioning to his glowing eyes.

"You were there! You were with me at the wreck! Leave me alone! No!"

Donald reached out his hand toward Jody, beckoning him to rise. "Remember me, Jody."

Jody scurried further away from Donald's grasp. He shielded his eyes from that glowing, piercing stare. "Who are you?" Jody screamed out a desperate demand.

Donald sighed and closed his eyes. The blazing gold and blue glow ceased, leaving both of them in the relative darkness of the lightly humming florescent lamps above. He rose and turned his back, his shoulders slumped in a loss of patience for this tiresome game.

"I am your friend, Jody."

Jody rose to his knees, ready to spring away as fast as his feet could take him. "No, you're the devil."

"I am not. Neither am I Santa Clause or the Easter Bunny." Donald glanced back at him over his shoulder, eyes no longer glowing. "Please, can we just move on?"

Jody rose to his feet. His shaking legs raced with adrenaline, begging him to loose them to retreat off into the night, but something inside him would not let them go. "Then... you are death."

"Please," Donald rolled his eyes and scoffed. "You give me far too much credit."

"Then you're..."

"Stop!" Donald turned and sternly raised his hand in protest. "No, I am not God. Don't speak that. Don't even think it." He looked around nervously. "I would not want to be told that my services are no longer necessary."

"But you do... work... for God?"

The old man nodded his head. "I've never made employee of the month, but I do my best." Jody was speechless. His mouth swung wide open and he stammered and stumbled. "I know, realizing I'm not just some Joe on the street can be shocking to most."

Jody found his words. "No... not you... it's just... there is... a God."

The old man frowned and looked over his shoulder. "Well, don't laugh in my ear like that. Yes, I know...humility." He coughed and gathered himself. "Like I said, not employee of the month."

"Was Allen..."

"No, he was human, flesh and bone and a gigantic broken heart. I was adopted into their family."

"But you were..."

"A fully grown man?" Donald chuckled. "I am what I need

to be, what *they* need me to be. Before, I looked like a child... now, I look like this."

"So, you can look like whatever you want?"

"Anything I *need* to look like." He smiled a big toothy grin. "I guess some poor soul needed *this*." He scratched at his beard, his big calloused hands tangling the strands of wiry hair. "...a bit itchy though."

"But Peter... Allen... me... what is it? Why us?"

"Peter and Allen, that's easy. *You*, I wondered myself for years. Normally, this is my territory, a few dozen blocks in a city in the Midwest, for over a hundred years I've worked this same beat. Lots of others were sent to much more interesting places, exotic places, fancy, sophisticated... I guess I shouldn't complain. I could be posted out in the middle of the ocean..."

"Don..."

"Yes?"

"You're rambling."

"Sorry. I've always had a problem. My heart is... two sizes too big...as they say. It's hard to do what I do and be so moved by compassion for... my clients."

"Your clients?"

"People... dying people."

"But...you're not death."

"Correct, I'm what comes just after death. I'm an usher, a Charon, a reaper. I take the souls of man to the next plane of existence."

"My father?"

"Yes... he was a remarkable man, kind, loving, his heart broke for you, for your pain, for leaving you so soon."

"I..."

Donald protested with an awkward deep throated cough. "Please, we really shouldn't talk about any more... the rules and all. Certain things aren't meant to be known, even by me... not yet."

The old man walked past Jody, clicking his way up the sidewalk. He beckoned the young man to follow with a flick of his wrist.

"But there is something you should know." He stopped and shoved his hands deep into the pockets of his slacks once again. His gaze lifted directly across the street, at the locked door of the old storefront he once called home. "How you... and Peter are connected."

There was a stirring behind the darkened windowpanes. Something shuffled amongst the bookcases, flitting quickly up and down the rows. Nothing was recognizable, no features, barely even a form, but it was there, and both of the men on the well-worn sidewalk knew it.

Donald watched, carefully, as he spoke, never blinking as he recounted the story to Jody.

"The thread that runs between you is my weakness. I was too weak to take Peter when the time came. I loved him, Allen loved him. His spirit stayed in that little townhouse, talking and playing with Allen every day. He wouldn't speak to me, and he told Allen who I really was. One night a demon came home with mother, latched on to her back like a cancer. It was feeding on her loneliness and pain. I couldn't take it off of her. She didn't want me to. That thing made self-pity a drug to her, so soothing and satisfying. It did the same with Peter. It was so easy in his unnatural state. It poisoned him, twisted him, until I couldn't even recognize him anymore. Hate begat hate, and darkness spiraled, pulling him... his remembrance of who and what he was...into the abyss. Allen couldn't let him go. I wanted to, but I couldn't break Allen's heart... not again."

The boy materialized inside, cold hand pressed against the glass, causing it to frost over in an unnatural print of a child's hand. There was no sound, but Donald could read his lips as the child mouthed "filio" so plainly, so clearly, even Jody had no doubt what was said.

The old man paused, a tear forming on the crown of his cheek. "Then... there was you, an amazing, beautiful boy, wrapped in the love of his father, not a care in the entire world. Through no fault of your own, your world turned upside down. Your father asked me to spare you, as I took his hand and pulled him into the bosom of the eternal. That was all the impetus I needed. I begged God to stay the hand of death." The tear streaked down his cheek. "And the hand of death passed over you."

Jody touched his palm to his chest and felt the beating pulse of his own heart. It pushed blood through his body, carrying oxygen and nutrients, cleaning out systems, and fulfilling all the necessary parts that made him human, made him who he was. It was the very stuff of life, handed down to him by his father. It was a life that he enjoyed, every day from that fateful morning until now, because of his father, because of Don.

"Thank you." He felt grateful and somehow ashamed and unworthy of such a gift.

"My mistakes have caused this, Jody." He gestured toward the cursed and poisoned building across the street. "All of my mercies, deaths deferred, have led to more pain, more suffering. It outweighs any good I have done."

Donald's words cut Jody to the bone. Don condemned his own actions, but Jody read within his words an indictment of himself. His drinking, his wasted life, all of his mistakes cried out to him from the depths of his past like wronged souls from mournful graves.

The old man closed his eyes once more and bowed his head. He nodded and on his downturned face, the faintest grateful smile turned the corners of his mouth.

"Yes, thank you." He whispered. "It is time."

When he lifted his head, his countenance was full of determination and his eyes began to glow with a golden gleam, ever so dimly, behind his deep blue-grey pools. "Tonight, we set right all that has gone wrong, and clear away all of those jagged, nasty pieces of the past."

Jody gulped. He had no experience resetting cosmic courses or setting right anything in the universe and thought perhaps he should start with tasks a bit more mundane.

"We?"

"You should know, this isn't going to be easy."

Jody gave the old man an indignant look. "You're kidding, right?"

"Not in the least." He took a perfectly pressed white hand-kerchief from his back pocket and offered it to the young man. "You look like you need this."

Jody took it from him with a trembling hand and patted the sweat that was beading on his brow. "How are you so... never mind."

"Demons are liars and manipulators. They can appear however they need to appear to suit their purpose. They can say whatever they need to say to suit their purpose. They need not speak the truth. Spirits speak from their own painful experi-ence, they appear as they did in their own lives, often stuck in the form in which they experienced death or some other major trauma. They cannot hurt you, but the demonic can, and both can manipulate you into hurting yourself."

"Sounds simple enough. Demons change, spirits don't, don't die." Jody tried to act nonchalant, but clearly this was all a bit much for him.

Donald nervously shuffled his feet upon realization of his friend's shocking level of incompetence. He had not anticipated all of this being so foreign to the young man.

"Fear and self-doubt have no place behind that door, Jody. They are fuel to the fires of hell and will consume you from the inside out."

Jody silently nodded. "And why am I doing this again?"

"Because you must." Donald snapped back.

His voice echoed through the empty street and shook the inside of Jody's ears. The young man did not understand but he dared not protest.

"Allen is dead. Peter is dead. Our mother is dead. They have lived their lives, made their choices. Once it is appointed for man to die, and then the judgement. I have to take Peter to his just reward, for better or worse, though I hope for the better. You are important here, because the battle still rages for your soul, and you decide the victor, within your own heart, within your own mind."

"My own heart? My own mind?" None of it made sense to Jody.

"Yes, yes, I know." Don whispered to some invisible force behind them.

"Forgiveness is a powerful gift, Jody. It is offered to you this day, from the hand of God himself." The old man rubbed his brow and spoke slowly and tenderly. He spoke of blood, of sacrifice, of an acceptance that defied logical understanding.

"It is a mystery to Heaven and Hell, offered to man alone. It is the seed of life, and the very substance of hope." Donald paced nervously. "Before you enter that building, Jody, you must accept this gift. It is shield and sword, armor against the deepest and darkest things this world and the other can throw at you."

"Forgiveness," the word was as foreign to Jody's tongue as the thought to his mind. "What do I do... for forgiveness?"

"The simple things... and the hard things." Donald smiled. "Accept it, put it on like a coat on a cold day. Then, forget; forget your past, your mistakes, and walk into the light free of the dark burdens fashioned by your own hand."

Jody pondered, trembling in the night mist. "Accept the pardon from beyond... and then... how am I supposed to just let all of that go, just like that. Everything I touch rots and dies. How am I supposed to just forgive...myself."

"The truth will set you free."

"Everyone I ever loved is rotting in their grave. I did that... I didn't stop it. I could have..."

"The truth will set you free."

Jody wept. Hot tears streamed down his face behind two spread palms that tried to hide his shame.

"It is a simple gift. Accept it, and the truth will set you free."

Time ticked imperceptibly past Jody's hidden face. He searched. He stretched and reached out within himself, trying to comprehend the simple gift he knew nothing about but knew he needed desperately.

"I...accept it." He groaned. "I don't understand... I don't... know... but I accept it."

Donald breathed deep and filled his barrel chest. "Rise, Jody. All you can do, is done."

Jody lowered his hands and looked into Donald's sparkling blue and golden eyes. The strange bald and bearded man held up three wrinkled but clearly muscular fingers in Jody's face.

"There are three things you must remember to survive the night, boy. You must not dwell on mistakes of the past. You must not allow the demon to touch you, and you must not yield to its lies. Do those three things and you may well not be dragged down into hell by the hair of your head."

The prospect of death was one thing, frightening, intimidating, but the prospect of hell was another realization entirely. Never had so much for him been weighed in the balance, and never had he felt so woefully unprepared for the task at hand.

Donald's shoes clicked once again against the hard pavement. He crossed the street and looked back toward Jody. "Well...are you coming?"

Jody wiped at his brow and lip one more time and carefully folded the handkerchief. With trembling palm, he slipped it into his pocket and addressed his coming fate.

"To see this thing done for once and for all? Of course, I am."

THIRTY-TWO

The lock turned. The door opened, and the old and the young entered a world of damnation and grief. Darkness filled the room, deep, palpable, and velvety. It swooshed around Jody's arms as he walked, pulling the hair straight up from his skin.

"The plan!?" He blurted.

"Please?" The old man scrunched his nose and squeaked his voice in confusion.

"What's the *plan*?" He tried to whisper and beckoned Donald to do the same.

He didn't know if keeping quiet voices would preserve any moniker of actual secrecy, but it seemed the thing to do.

"Listen, I'm sure setting things right like this is commonplace for you..."

"Hardly..."

That answer brought Jody no comfort, but he continued on anyway. "But I need some kind of direction."

The old man winced and rolled his eyes. "I've already told you. Don't die. I handle both of them, Peter first, and you, just... don't... die."

"Okay, that's... a good plan." Jody shifted his weight in his shoes as if preparing for some great physical contest. "You take Peter first... and I... don't... die. Wait... that means I have to take on the demon first? I can't beat a demon."

Donald let out an exasperated wheeze. "You have got to be... I've already told you before, the three things. Look, we can't do this if I have to keep repeating myself over and over."

The final movement of the Stabat Mater wafted through the darkness, and a boy's laugh echoed around the room.

"Peter is the trickier of the two. He requires a... special touch. I will handle him, alone. And Jody, don't die." A sly smile peaked through the long beard. The instructions were simple, but Jody was still completely at a loss as to their execution.

Donald stepped off into the darkness, leaving Jody behind surrounded by a coal black fog. A brilliant blue and gold light blazed behind the veil, moving back and forth. Inaudible words were uttered and suddenly, the hazy vesper of light disappeared, swallowed by the black of Jody's surroundings.

"Donald? Where are you man?" he called out into the night.

No answer returned to him on the wind, only the chilling sense of a vague evil muddled with the acrid smell of stale coffee.

A deep and gravelly voice split the darkened cloud around the young man and rattled his brain. "Jody... Jody... I see you."

It transformed syllable by syllable into that of a quivering old woman and the veil around them slowly evaporated. "I see you, my little sweet boy."

The room around them was empty, dimly illuminated by soft and warm lamplight. "I want you."

In the corner, hands carefully clasped at her waist, stood a wrinkled woman in a vintage dress. Gracefully, on gliding steps, she closed the gap between them.

"I could just eat you right up." A wiry, shriveled tongue lapped at her lips.

Donald's voice drifted aimlessly amongst the rafters,

barking some long poetic command, but Jody could not make out any of the words. The woman before him growled from deep within her throat. The rumbling deep male voice returned.

"Remember, old man, I can still do two things at once."

She smacked her flapping jowls and Jody, took three shaky steps back. She reached out her hand towards the young man and begged him for just a touch of his hand.

It drew him in, muscles processing involuntarily. He moved without thought, without will, like a moth to a flame. His hand rose, eyes fixated on the spindly shriveled outstretched finger. The demon laughed for joy, perceiving Jody's dulling intellect. Jody drifting into dream and nothingness, eyes rolling back into his head, hand outstretched. The beast salivated for the taste of souls.

"No!" Jody pulled his hand away, blinking hard and shaking himself. "You can't! I won't let you."

The old woman screamed and raised her hands toward heaven. She pulled apart atom by atom in a stream of vile gore, howling and writhing. A flash of brilliant light pulsed through the room. She was no more.

Jody was surrounded by nothingness as a thick black fog settled in amongst the bookshelves and surrounded him. It cloaked his senses, all but consumed him.

"Your permission means nothing, you filthy wretch." The deep voice boomed from within the veil.

Jody choked on the thick darkness. It clogged his throat and tickled his lungs. He teetered on weakening legs, losing all sense of balance. His body was racked with heaving coughs, air forced from deep within his diaphragm, droplets of saliva and mucus ripping at his raspy throat. He heaved over and over again.

Jody gasped in with a great airy groan. Fresh air filled his chest, the fog was gone, the atmosphere in the room clear and bright.

"Donald?... Don? Did you see that?" Jody waited but heard nothing in reply except the echo of his own voice.

A single drop of water fell from ceiling to floor and crossed his vision, landing with a loud and pronounce plop before him. Jody leaned in and studied the curious, fluid pattern of scattered and beaded water droplets left behind. They faded and drew in to the dry and aged wooden boards beneath his feet. As he crouched, mesmerized, watching the water dance and sink into the floor, he felt a gentle drop land on the back of his head. Instinctively he wiped it away with his hand. The cold water mingled in his hair and wet his palm. Jody gazed up to the ceiling looking for a stain or beading water course, some telltale sign of a leak.

Another drop fell from nowhere, splashing onto his forehead. Jody blinked instinctively. Another hit his nose, and quickly another on his cheek. The popcorn report of hundreds, then thousands of drops of water, falling on the old wooden floor surrounded him, water now freely flowing down his skin and clothes, soaking him to the bone. Thunder rumbled and shook the old storefront. Jody wiped his eyes dry as best he could, struggling to bring the world back in to focus.

The dark and shadowy figure of a man emerged from the corner of the room and made its way toward Jody, through the beating rain, his halting footsteps sloshing across the floor in an awkward rhythm. "I want to talk to you." The cold and quivering voice sounded somehow familiar.

"Who are you?"

"I want to talk to you." The dark figure grew more insistent. "Why did you bring that gun?"

The figure became clearer, a dark hood was pulled down close over his face. Jody couldn't distinguish his features, but he knew. He could never forget the piercing eyes behind that thick wet cloth.

"I just wanted to talk to you, Jody. I just wanted to tell you I was sorry!" The sorrow filled voice echoed from the walls.

Jody stumbled back as the dark man drew closer. "It's not my fault...not my fault!"

The figure stopped. "It's your's Jody, take it. Don't you want it?" The figure's arm stretched out toward Jody, and in his hand, dripping with blood mingled with water, he held the handgun. The familiar wooden handle hung in the air, waiting to be grasped by Jody's warm hand.

He could take it. It was his, the legacy left to him by his father. He could touch it. He could feel its weight in his palm. He could know it once more, count on it to work, always, when needed. He could lower it on the target. It was his. He could squeeze the smooth trigger and when the hammer fell, he would have vengeance. He would have an end to it all, to the pain, to the struggle, to the nightmares. It would all be over. He just had to take it.

Jody's hand tingled. It felt weak, empty, wanting. "It's mine."

"Take it." The figure stepped once more toward Jody.

Jody wiped the rain from his brow and shifted nervously in his shoes. He flexed the fingers of his right hand. They were becoming numb. He cradled them in his left. They felt cold, and lifeless. "It's mine," he repeated through clinched teeth.

His heart broke. Tears welled up in his eyes, and he whimpered softly under his breath.

"I can take it!"

He wanted to. He wanted to unclasp his hands and take the familiar grip of his father's gun in his hands, but he could not. His heart sped. There was a war deep within his chest. The cold hand of death pricked at his skin and beckoned him to yield, begged him to claim what was rightfully his.

"Take it, Jody. Just take it," the dark figure hissed.

"I... can't." He wretched and groaned. "It's killing me."

"It's your's. Take it!"

"If I take it... it's going to kill me."

"No it won't, Jody. Take it. End it, Jody. End it all. YOU killed me with this! YOU destroyed me, Jody, because I hurt you. Now I want you."

He shivered in the cold rain, and pulled his dying hand up to his chest. "No, no I didn't."

"Don't you feel any shame, Jody? Don't you feel any regret? I would still be here, Jody! My kids would still have a dad, if you hadn't dropped this gun, Jody!"

The gun slipped from the dark man's hand and crashed onto the floor with a resounding thud. "Pick it up! Take it! End it, Jody! End it! End it now!"

"No, I can't... I just can't," Jody whimpered. "No! I can't... I won't," he barked back. "It's not my fault! It's not my fault!"

The dark man lunged for Jody, his outstretched neck freeing his face from the concealment of the hood. He screamed in Jody's face, his hot breath washing over Jody, wreaking of decay. He drew back his fist as if to strike, but in the last moment thrust his hand toward the ground and picked up the weapon. The monster snarled at Jody, eyes cold and glassy, covered in cataracts, his face eaten with the rot and decay of the grave, the gaping hole from the exit wound still visible in the dim light. The dark man snarled, raised the gun to his own temple and pulled the trigger, collapsing to the floor.

Nothingness returned. Jody was utterly enveloped in warm darkness. All was silence, there was no more rain, and he didn't even feel wet anymore. He became aware he was laying on the floor near the door, flat on his back.

"Don?... Don?... H-help me, please."

Slowly he rose. Don was nowhere to be found, but he was not alone. In the back of the store, leaning against a bookcase, clothed in a flowing red silk negligee, thumbing wistfully through a dime store novel, stood a beautiful fair-skinned woman. Her red hair bounced in tight, perfectly primmed curls. She bit at her lusciously red lower lip, eyes creeping up to catch a glimpse of her one-time lover.

"Karen?" The rest of existence fell to the wayside. He was utterly entranced by her. "Are you…"

"Real?" she giggled. "As real as anything else you've ever touched…or tasted."

She meticulously returned the book exactly where she took it from, allowing her fingertips to ride seductively down its spine, giving a gentle groan of approval as it was finally seated in place.

"I've… missed you, so much." An aching gnawed at his heart. It was hungry. He felt light, dizzy, empty, like he had wasted away to skin and bones.

"Come here, love," she purred, laying aside her book. "I am yours for the taking."

He walked slowly towards her; each step halting, each foot-fall singing with anticipation, with warm excitement, and with pain. As he approached, he could smell her sweet perfume. He breathed it in deeply, consumed it utterly like a luscious meal.

"I had forgotten that," he whispered.

"There is oh so much you have forgotten, my dear. Come and see. I have so much to show you."

She stretched a long naked thigh out toward him and traced the curves of her body with her fingertip from hip to ankle and back again.

"I am yours. I want you."

He reached for her. His arm tingled with want and desire. He remembered what her skin felt like beneath his fingertips. In his mind, he was already touching her, consumed in the memory of their first night together. He gasped as he felt the same waves of pleasure. He was consumed by the memory.

Jody fell prostrate to the floor, unable to separate that which was from that which is.

Karen clucked in disapproval. "Naughty boy," she pouted. She approached his limp body, shifting her weight from hip to hip. "Come on, Jody, wake up."

She kneeled beside him and drew her lips so close to his ear, they almost grazed his hair. "Wake up, my precious, precious boy," she whispered. "Wake up, Jody. Jody, time to wake up."

Her sing-song voice centered his tumultuous thoughts. He stirred and groaned. Hands unfurled and with quivering sinew he rose to his knees.

"Karen... I..."

"Jody, please," she begged breathlessly. "I need you. I need to feel you... I need..."

He squinted hard. Jody wanted to give her everything she wanted, to experience it all once again. He wanted to touch her, but something deep down inside fought to restrain him.

It was a memory, dark, distant. Something from the past nagged at his consciousness, just out of reach. It buzzed and flitted, louder and louder, until it could no longer be ignored.

Karen was dead. He had buried her, laid two white roses on her redwood casket and cried as the first fist full of earth slipped through his fingers and fell into the depths of her grave to dance upon the lid.

"Please, my love. I beg you. Touch me."

"No!" He recoiled back.

"Touch me!" Her voice cracked and hissed like a serpent mid-strike.

Canine teeth gleamed in the lamplight as she lunged for him. Then, nothing. The world was consumed in blinding light.

Jody shielded his eyes. His hands burned from the brilliance of the light around him, but the shadow of their station granted him space and relieve enough to open his eyelids.

There, in the corner of the room, the silhouette of a little boy lifted its arms toward heaven and shot up like lightning through the ceiling. A concussive pulse radiated from the shadowy figure and knocked Jody back, hard against the ancient wooden floorboards. His head bounced, the world span around him, and his mind cramped and ached, pulling his entire being to the center of the earth.

Jody fought the urge to sleep, to close his eyes and dream himself somewhere anywhere other than this strange, accursed room.

"Donald...help me!" He murmured, for that was all that he could manage, every ounce of strength and breath within him, pushed through his mouth in a final plea for help.

Above him hovered a being, whether founded in the physical or metaphysical realm, it was impossible for Jody to tell.

Every fiber of its body glowed a warm and golden hue, like burnished brass. Its form was human but with three sets of wings springing from its back, but only one pair of wings flapped slowly back and forth, keeping the being suspended somewhere between heaven and earth.

Its face could not be seen, exuding such brilliant, undying, and burning light that it physically burned Jody's face as he tried to look upon it. In form, the being was beautiful, but somehow Jody felt an evil energy emanating from it. The being reached down towards Jody, but could not reach him, constrained by some unseen force. It called out in the same low and gravelly voice Jody had heard before.

"He is mine! I own him! I want him! Let me have him you pitiful human."

"Oh, how the mighty have fallen." Donald's voice was crisp and clear, echoing as if from a loudspeaker in the middle of the now relatively small room. Clicking footsteps approached the young man, stopping near his head.

Looming over him, stood the same figure he had known these long months. An aging, dignified man, balded shiny head perched atop a noble black beard, every feature of his face exactly as Jody had always known him, but now his skin glowed, golden and bright.

He looked down and offered Jody the slightest smile and then steeled his face and looked back up at the winged celestial creature hovering above them.

The winged one scoffed at Donald. "Who are you to mock me? You have no power here."

It skittered about moving this way and that across the ceiling in midair, as if foot and hand were dragging its immense body across some unseen elevated floor. "Are you God, that I should tremble and flee at your power in all of its cold and unjust majesty?"

"I am not... blasphemer."

In a flash of motion, the great golden being cocked its head to the side and craned its neck, leaning hard to take in a better look. "I know who you are." The growling voice thinned into almost a hiss. "You are Donald Longworth, the other child. Why would you come back here?"

"I come as I am sent. Leave the boy alone." Donald snapped, grinding one well-shoed heel into the floor.

The winged-one leaned in even closer, still clinging to some unseen shelf with all four limbs. "I will not, and you cannot stop me." A smile flashed across his golden face. "Do you even know my name? It is ancient and unpronounceable to your carnal imperfect tongue, older than the foundation of the world, more ancient than the farthest star. You are no match for my power and splendor. Leave before I crush you like a maggot under foot."

The bearded man took three long steps forward. "Donald Longworth is not the name I was given. It is the name I have taken. My name, my true name, though not as ancient, is just as unpronounceable as your own."

Jody trembled as his eyes beheld the being behind the voice of his acquaintance. It came from something altogether different from the aging man with a bald head and long black beard he knew. Grounding him to the floor were long, muscular legs ending in cloven hooves, like calf's feet. His body was altogether human, not old and withered, but perfectly formed, and on his back, two great sets of wings. All of his being was golden and glowing just like the thing that hovered above them.

His face was not consumed by a fiery light, but it blurred and transformed, twitching and flashing from one form to the next. Always between the same four forms. First, was the face of a man, remarkably similar to what a younger, stronger Donald would have looked like were he well-shaven. Second, was the face of a lion, growling and terrible. Next, the face of an Ox, strong and stern, and finally, that of an eagle, noble and fierce.

As the being spoke, what first appeared as a glistening or a sparkle of its skin, became not a shimmer or a sparkle, but the random blinking of thousands of eyes, that covered the being from body to wing. "He belongs to no one. The breath of life still fills his lungs. He is not yours to take."

The winged one above them laughed loudly. "I know what you are. You are nothing, a child, nothing but a servant. You were created after me and you were formed beneath me. I will not give this one up, neither is he yours to keep, reaper of the dead. Servant of the most high taskmaster. Know your place lowly one." It growled and spat flaming tongues of light where its mouth should be.

Donald's wings beat furiously behind him. "Hold your tongue."

The six-winged creature turned its head and flew down close to Donald with a motion that more closely resembled a slither than flight. "I existed for eons before you were first spoken into existence. Who are you to command me?"

"I stand in the office given to me by the Most High, proclaimed before the throne amongst the assembly of the sons of God. You know who I am, and you know I hold the word of the Father. Go, while you can."

"The Father," the flying being hissed. "You would call him that wouldn't you, worm." The being swooshed down toward Jody and swiped at him. His hand bounced and flew back once it was only a few inches from Jody's face. He screamed, and the room shook around them for the force of the sound.

"Remove the hedge, maggot!"

"I cannot." Donald chuckled. "It is not my hedge. I did not place it."

The brazen beast flew back into an upper corner of the room and sulked its hulking body like a cowering dog. He snapped and snarled back at them. "Hear me, servant of the unjust one, this filthy pile of dung would not choose to cower before the light as you did. He would choose his own way, every time, just like I did. He is broken and double-minded. Let him crawl to me."

"Half-truths and games of shadow. He could crawl to you any time he so desires, but he does not so desire. He seeks the light."

Donald reached beneath an open palm and materialized a blue and golden censer, made of a substance like lapis lazuli. It fell from his hand and stopped at the end of a long golden chain, which Donald clasped in his hand. He swung it, to and fro. From it emanated a great blue cloud of smoke, and filled Jody's nostrils with a sweet, sweet smell. "Your time has been counted and is now finished here."

Donald drew up the chain and held the smoking censer in both his hands. He lifted it up to his mouth and spoke softly words that Jody instinctively felt meant something deep and ancient, but which he could not interpret or understand.

The smoke reached out like a spectral arm from the censer, guided by the breath of Donald's words. The six-winged creature howled and gnashed against fate. It beat the walls with fists and wing. The building shook once more, walls cracked and books tumbled to the earth. When the smoke reached the beast, a brilliant light pulsed and a crash like thunder tore through Jody's ears. The young man was shoved once more, hard against the floor and felt himself slipping again, off into the world of dreams and shadow.

"It is over, my friend." Donald's voice snapped Jody's consciousness back from the warm cradle of dark nothingness.

Jody was standing in the darkened front room of the Study Hall. He pawed at his forearms and face, not believing entirely that what he had experienced was reality, but skin felt skin, warm and full of life. It was real, and he made it through.

Along the wall, Jody heard the click of a lamp. There, in the lamplight, beside a broken bookcase and shambled pile of books, stood an aged bald and bearded man. "Jody, you didn't die."

"I guess not," the corners of his mouth upturned in a light and sincere smile. "But you were..."

"Who I've always been." Donald's eyes glowed blue and gold as he walked over to his friend, in his familiar bald and bearded form. "It's time, Jody."

"Time for what?"

Donald closed his eyes and when he opened them again, they were the deep blue-grey Jody was accustomed to. "There is only one thing left to do, and then the world will be set back to the way it was, before I caused such a mess." The old man offered Jody his hand.

"But don't I get a choice?"

Donald drew his hand back. "It is appointed for man once to die, and then...".

Normally man has no choice in the day or hour of his death. The day is appointed, the hour chosen, and they are ushered to their judgement and eternity. Don had broken that rule long ago, giving ear to man in his moment of weakness, taking action on their behalf. In some way, Jody was the child of choice, the son of a man not afraid to reach out beyond what should be and dare to touch what could have been.

"Speak."

"I want to stay. I'm not ready to go yet."

"Jody, you don't understand. There is so much more pain, so much more hurt out there for you if you stay." He reached out his hand once more.

Jody rejected it. "I want to stay. There is so much more out there that I want to do, to know. All of that joy, all of that happiness... I think it might be worth the pain."

Donald looked over his shoulder for a moment, listening to an unheard voice. He sighed. "I understand." He held out two upturned palms.

"The choice is yours, Jody, life or death."

CHAPTER
THIRTY-THREE

Time passed. Days, months, years paraded past, pulling Jody along with them. He lived. He breathed. Choices, dreams, goals, were all chased and marked meticulously across a pile of annual calendars, each crossed with black x's and checks until their pages were all but blotted out and discarded in turn.

Now was another year, another summer, and another family event at a small country church along an ancient, wooded ridge, not too far from the Red River he once ran with his father as a child.

A small boy played a game of ball with a friend in thick green grass underneath a blazing and happy mid-day sun. He kicked the giant red ball back and forth between himself and his friend, continually fighting with his pair of black dress pants, pulling them up around the stomach of his formerly white and well-pressed dress shirt.

The child giggled as the ball returned to him from his friend's bounding kick. It glanced off of his arm as he tried, unsuccessfully, to cradle it to a stop. The red orb ricocheted wildly and bounced twice, leaping over the thick luxurious lawn and onto the hot table of asphalt of a parking lot filled to the brim with cars of all kinds and descriptions. He chased it, trying to match pace and pitch as it moved further and further from his grasp, until it stopped.

The giant red ball found rest in the sturdy experienced hands of a grown man. The boy stopped and looked. He had never seen this curious man before. Several other similarly clothed children came to the boy's side, running and giggling, straining up through raised hands shielding them from the brilliant sunlight to see the man's face. Each came to a silent stop, mouths agape, staring the strange and curious man holding the giant red ball.

They watched the ball bouncing gayly between his fingertips. The man wore a perfectly pressed pin-striped suit, a wide, inviting smile, and a long black beard beneath a freshly shaven brow. One of the boys made silent petition raising two upturned palms toward the bouncing red orb. The man laughed and gently tossed the ball into the arms of the young boy.

In a flash, the boys had turned and gone, running back to the crowd of people gathering around steps of the white country church. The bells rang, and conversation murmured and babbled all around. Blankets were being spread. Baskets were being gathered, a bounty of home cooked food, emerging from every trunk and back seat in the parking lot.

Down those well-worn church steps came an aged man with a white mustache, steadying himself between the black handrail and the ever-present arm of his wife, her wrinkled cocoa skin accented by her beautiful white laced dress.

"Papaw! Papaw! Look!" The little boy tugged at his grandfather's pants, nearly knocking him off balance. The old man chuckled.

"What is it?"

"Look!" The little boy pointed, begging his grandfather to look out toward the parking lot.

The old man looked. Even through straining and aging eyes,

he could make out the bald and bearded man, smiling widely, waving at him in the distance. Jody laughed loudly and let go of the railing to wave hello boisterously, with all of his might. He waved so wildly that he threw himself off balance and would have fallen, had it not been for the steadying effort of his wife.

"Oh dear!" she exclaimed. "Who did you see?"

He looked back toward the parking lot and the bearded man was gone without a trace. The old man chuckled and hummed to himself reflectively.

"Oh, no one, Meg, just an old friend. I'll see him soon, I'm sure."

About the Author

James Carl Meadows began life amongst the rugged ridges, cliffs, and valleys of Kentucky's Red River Gorge, along the Sheltowee Trace. He grew strong and proud, nurtured by friends and family, beneath the emerald canopy of the Daniel Boone National Forrest. He graduated from Morehead State University, where he fell in love with the writing of regional masters like Jesse Stuart. Once a man, degree in hand and wife by his side, he followed the rolling brown waters of the Licking River up to its confluence with the Ohio. Between the courses of those two ancient waterways, he found a place to settle down and bring the stories out of his imagination and onto the page. His writing reflects the storytelling traditions of his Scotch-Irish roots, flavored by other nationally known influences like Patrick Rothfuss, M. L. Wang, Brandon Sanderson, and more. Now, for the first time, he has written down one of those stories from his dreams, to be enjoyed by all who would pull up a chair, pick up a book, and join him on a literary adventure.

PRAISE FOR COFFEE, SECRETS, CINCINNATI

"A thought-provoking story about the exploration of the paranormal and the journey of salvation." – Danielle Valdez, author

"A modern day ghost story, skillfully written to keep you guessing and turning the pages." — Paula Allen, author

www.ingramcontent.com/pod-product-compliance
Lightning Source LLC
Chambersburg PA
CBHW050314110726
47899CB00007B/2234